Amy tossed her hair back. "I've invited *tons* of people," she said loudly. Johanna felt as if Amy were staring straight at her. "*Everyone's* coming," she repeated.

"Come on, Amy, let's get out of here," Jean whispered.

"Oh, all right," said Amy. "I have to meet Peter anyway. He just goes *insane* if I'm late."

The four girls walked out of the library, leaving Johanna alone to study. It was no good, though; she couldn't concentrate. All she could think about was Amy's party on Friday night and the PTA dance. She imagined Amy and Peter slow dancing together, and a lump formed in her throat. Finally she gathered her things together and hurried out of the library.

To her surprise, Amy and her friends were standing just outside the door, still talking animatedly. Peter had joined them and was listening to something Amy was telling him. He barely looked up as Johanna walked past.

He acted as if he hadn't seen her, as if she didn't exist. *Because I don't exist for him,* Johanna thought numbly, her eyes filling with tears. *I was out of my mind to think it could possibly be different.*

Bantam Books in the Sweet Valley High Series
Ask your bookseller for the books you have missed

SWEET VALLEY HIGH

LAST CHANCE

Written by
Kate William

Created by
FRANCINE PASCAL

BANTAM BOOKS
TORONTO · NEW YORK · LONDON · SYDNEY · AUCKLAND

RL 6, IL age 12 and up

LAST CHANCE
A Bantam Book / May 1987

Sweet Valley High is a registered trademark of Francine Pascal.

Conceived by Francine Pascal.

Produced by Cloverdale Press, Inc.

Cover art by James Mathewuse.

ISBN 0-553-26478-8

Published simultaneously in the United States and Canada

Bantam Books are published by Bantam Books, Inc. Its trademark,
consisting of the words "Bantam Books" and the portrayal of a rooster,
is Registered in U.S. Patent and Trademark Office and in other
countries. Marca Registrada. Bantam Books, Inc., 666 Fifth Avenue,
New York, New York 10103.

LAST CHANCE

One

"Is it my imagination," Jessica Wakefield asked, her blue-green eyes sparkling as she set her tray down across the table from her friend, Cara Walker, "or is the cafeteria food even worse than usual this week?"

"They're trying to starve us," Winston Egbert said gloomily, an expression of mock anguish on his face as he peered underneath his soggy hamburger bun.

Winston, a tall, lanky boy with a spattering of freckles across the bridge of his nose, was the self-appointed clown of the junior class at Sweet Valley High. And the cafeteria food was a favorite subject for his jokes.

Jessica giggled. "Well, at least it makes it easy to diet," she said cheerfully, pushing her tray away and leaning forward to talk to Cara. "I found the most fantastic dress at the mall yesterday," she confided, "but they only have a size four. It's absolutely perfect for the PTA dance—

1

it's all sort of bare and filmy and everything—so I figure if I can lose about three or four pounds and if I don't eat anything the day of the dance . . ."

Cara giggled. "Thank goodness they didn't just have a size sixteen left, or you'd have to eat a dozen hamburgers a day between now and the dance to grow into it!"

Jessica tossed back her silky, sun-streaked blond hair and grimaced. The thought of gaining weight was all she needed to lose her appetite completely. Not that Jessica—a model-slim, perfect size six—ever had to worry about her weight. But she was fanatic about her appearance, and the PTA dance was one of the biggest events to be held at the school in a long time.

"Who are you going with?" Cara asked curiously, taking a sip of milk.

Jessica wrinkled her nose. "I don't know." She sighed. "Honestly, I'm so sick of all the guys around here." She lowered her voice, making sure Winston was concentrating on his conversation with his girlfriend, Maria Santelli, before she continued. "You know what I mean? They're all so . . . I don't know. *Boring*." She looked thoughtfully around the crowded cafeteria. "I may ask Rob Atkins, that guy from Bridgewater High I met at the soccer game. Remember?"

Cara nodded as she picked up her sandwich. "I'm glad Steve's going to be in town," she remarked. "I don't know what I'd do if I couldn't go with him. I can't think of a single guy at Sweet Valley High I'd feel like going with, either."

Jessica's eyes clouded over briefly. Cara had been her friend for ages, and at first Jessica had been overjoyed when Cara started dating Steven, Jessica's eighteen-year-old brother. In fact Jessica had tried her hardest to get the two of them together. She thought Cara was exactly what Steven needed. Now . . . she wasn't so sure. For some time she'd been growing increasingly uneasy about her friend Cara. It seemed to Jessica that Cara was getting way too dependent on Steven, and vice versa. Fortunately Jessica thought, Steven lived in a dorm at the state university where he was a freshman. That meant that Cara didn't get to see him every weekend. But the next week Steven would be at home for a break. As much as she loved her brother, Jessica didn't want Cara to count on Steven too much. She felt Cara should be more independent.

Jessica decided she wasn't going to encourage Cara one bit, not even by talking with her about the dance if Cara was going to drag Steven into it. She was relieved when she heard a familiar voice hailing her.

"Jess! Can I come over and join you guys?"

Winston and Maria looked up from their conversation, and Winston grinned as Elizabeth hurried over, plopped down into a chair, and pulled a brown paper lunch bag out of her nylon

3

backpack. "Look," he said to Maria with a mischievous smile. "It's Jessica's better half!"

Jessica ignored him. For as long as she could remember, she and Elizabeth had put up with being teased about being identical twins. But they had both gotten used to it long ago, and the truth was that neither minded. Anyway, as far as "identical" went, their likeness was all on the surface. It was almost impossible for strangers to tell them apart. Both had pretty, oval faces framed with shoulder-length, sun-kissed blond hair. The only physical difference between the girls was the tiny mole on Elizabeth's right shoulder.

But when it came to personality; Well in *that* department the twins were entirely different. Elizabeth liked to remind her sister that she was four minutes older, and sometimes those four minutes felt like years! Elizabeth was as organized and dependable as her twin was haphazard and flighty. It was typical, for example, that Elizabeth had thought ahead the night before and had made herself a sandwich for lunch. Jessica could never plan so far in advance. She lived for the moment, throwing herself heart and soul into whatever activity absorbed her that week. Elizabeth often accused her of being fickle, but from Jessica's point of view, it was just that she loved variety, and having a good time. She couldn't see the point in limiting herself to a single boy, the way Elizabeth did. She had been going out with Jeffrey French for a while. Jessica preferred playing the field. Things that really counted to Jessica, such as cheerleading and the exclusive sorority of which she was president, were allotted a certain amount of time. Whatever was left over was for having fun.

Elizabeth was much more serious and steady. Her lifelong dream was to be a writer, and she hoped the long hours she had logged at *The Oracle*, Sweet Valley High's student newspaper, would help her toward that end. She genuinely loved to study, something Jessica found baffling. And though she liked to enjoy herself as much as her twin did, Elizabeth's favorite pasttimes were reading, listening to music, and having long talks with her best friend, Enid Rollins, or Jeffrey. Jessica couldn't understand Elizabeth's feeling on either count. Enid Rollins seemed to Jessica to be the dullest girl in the school, and nothing Elizabeth said in her defense could change her mind. Jeffrey was OK; in fact, Jessica thought he was pretty cute. But she couldn't see the point in getting tied down so soon. First Cara, now Elizabeth, she thought, sighing. What *was* it that could make a sixteen-year-old girl want to ruin her social life by going out with only one guy?

"I'm so excited about Steven's coming home," Elizabeth declared, glancing at her sister's untouched tray and offering her half of her sandwich.

Jessica accepted automatically, forgetting about

5

the dress at the mall and her resolve to diet. "Thanks," she said, taking a bite and wishing Elizabeth had chosen another subject. Sure enough, Cara's face lit up, and within seconds she and Elizabeth were going on and on about Steven's wonderful qualities. Jessica frowned. This wasn't the way to make Cara realize she needed to broaden her horizons. But then what was?

"Hi, guys!" Amy Sutton called, pulling a chair up to their table and helping herself to Jessica's untouched french fries. "These are gross," she said, continuing to eat them anyway. "I bet you're all wondering whether or not I'm still going to have a predance party at my house next week, aren't you?"

"Anticipation," Winston declared, "has us all breathless."

Maria giggled and put her hand restrainingly on Winston's arm. "We *were* wondering," she said. Maria, Jessica, Cara, and Amy were all on the cheerleading squad, so Amy had already talked to the other three about the party.

Amy Sutton was a pretty blond girl with a slightly haughty expression in her sky-blue eyes and an attitude that seemed to suggest everyone should drop what he or she was doing the minute she approached the table. Back in sixth grade, she and Elizabeth had been best friends, but after the Suttons moved to the East Coast, the friendship slowly faded. This year Amy's family moved back to Sweet Valley, and Elizabeth discovered that Amy had changed. Even Jessica was beginning to admit that Amy could be a pain, and Jessica had been her biggest champion, working hard to get her on the cheerleading squad and listening with delight to Amy's endless stories about boys.

"Of course, this party is going to be a really big deal for Peter and me," Amy added, as if this were obvious. She helped herself to Jessica's hamburger without asking. "I mean, it's the first party we'll be—you know—*giving together*."

"Peter?" Elizabeth said blankly. The last she knew, Amy was chasing after an intern who worked at her mother's TV station.

"Peter DeHaven," Jessica filled in for her. "He and Amy have been going out."

"Peter DeHaven?" Elizabeth repeated. She had to catch herself to avoid displaying the surprise she was feeling. She had been one second away from blurting out, "But he's so smart!" That was what everyone said about Peter DeHaven. And it was true; he was one of the brightest guys in the school. Elizabeth didn't know him very well, as Peter was a senior and had been enrolled in special science classes from the day he entered high school. She knew he'd been admitted early to MIT, and had won every prize for science there was, except the coveted Southern California Science Fair, which he was rumored to be entering that month. He was a tall, attractive, serious-looking boy with dark hair and hazel eyes—a well-liked, hard-working guy who happened to be an ace tennis player as well as a top-notch science student. Elizabeth couldn't imagine what he and Amy Sutton had in common. What on earth could they talk about together? she wondered.

As if reading her mind, Amy began to launch into an extravagant description of their romance. "Peter's mad about me," she confided, unwrapping a brownie and taking a bite. "In fact, I'm getting a little nervous." She giggled. "I mean, he *is* older and everything. And you know how *serious* he is."

"I never really thought Peter was your type, Amy," Cara said calmly, giving Jessica and Elizabeth a wink. "Isn't he kind of—I don't know—kind of a workaholic?"

Amy looked indignant. "Not at all! Peter's just good at everything he does. He can't help being a superstar, can he?"

"No," Cara said soothingly, "he can't. I just meant, are you really all that compatible? I didn't think you were interested in science."

"Science," Amy repeated, as if it were a foreign word. "Oh, well, I'm not," she conceded. "I think it's about the most boring thing in the world. But Peter's *adorable*. And he never talks about any of that stuff when we're together. I wouldn't let him, even if he tried. We talk about *fun* things—like the party next week," she concluded dreamily. "You know, stuff like *that*."

Jessica was about to ask another question when Winston cut her off. "Look, there's Julie," he said, getting to his feet and waving to the petite, red-haired junior who was balancing her lunch tray and looking around her in confusion. Julie Porter and Winston had become friendly during the past few weeks, after working together on a project for Cabaret Night. Julie was a talented musician, but she had always been shy about her piano playing. No one had known how good she was before she played at Cabaret Night, and Winston was still full of admiration every time he saw her.

Everyone made room at the table so Julie could pull up a chair. "Thanks," she said shyly, setting down her tray. She gave Winston a grateful smile. Julie was somewhat of a loner, perhaps because she spent long hours practicing. She was well-liked at school, but few people knew her well. Watching her now, Elizabeth remembered what good friends they had been in the sixth grade.

Though they had once been close, Elizabeth knew little more than the brief outlines of the Porter family's history. She knew that Julie and her older sister, Johanna, were the children of professional musicians. Mr. Porter played violin for the Los Angeles Symphony, and Mrs. Porter, before her tragic death over six months before, had been a well-known opera singer. The girls had traveled a great deal in summers and, when necessary, had been taken out of school. Julie had adjusted to their unusual lifestyle with little difficulty. She worked hard and

9

did fairly well in all her courses, though as she grew older, most of her time was reserved for one great love—the piano.

But Johanna, who should have been a senior that year, had a much harder time. Elizabeth didn't know the inside story. All she knew was that Johanna Porter had always been in academic trouble. She got C's and D's in almost every class, was constantly on probation, and seemed to suffer through each assignment. The previous year, about six months before Mrs. Porter was killed in a car crash, Johanna withdrew from school. At first no one could believe she was serious. What would she do without a high-school diploma? Everyone assumed she would change her mind, but she didn't. Johanna had decided to drop out, and that was that. But the very latest news was that Johanna was coming back. Robin Wilson had told Jessica so just the other day, and thanks to Jessica, the rumor had spread like wildfire.

"I guess you've all heard the news," Julie said now, taking a deep breath as she faced the crowd at the table.

"What news?" Winston asked curiously.

Julie looked nervously around the table. "You haven't heard?" she asked. "I thought for sure it would be all over the place by now."

"I haven't heard anything," Winston declared. "What's happened, Julie?"

"It's Johanna," Julie said, trying to make her voice sound natural. She took another deep breath. "She's decided to come back to school, to give it another chance."

Winston and Maria were the only ones at the table who hadn't heard the news, and clearly both were astonished.

"Today's her first day," Julie continued matter-of-factly. "She's in the office right now, filling out all the forms." She paused. "She's going to be a junior again, so she'll be in some of your classes," she added.

"Wow," Amy said, licking some chocolate off her finger. "I think I'd just *die* of mortification if my sister—"

"Amy," Elizabeth hissed, cutting her off. "*I* think it's great," she said quickly, hoping to cover up Amy's rudeness. "Johanna must have a lot of courage. I bet it isn't easy starting over again."

"I don't think it is," Julie said quietly. Her expression serious, she looked around the table. "And I think we're all going to have to do what we can to help her. Otherwise . . ."

Julie never finished her sentence, but Elizabeth could feel the portent of what was left unsaid. They were going to have to help Johanna, she thought. Otherwise, the girl would never make it through school.

Two

Johanna Porter was in the girls' bathroom at the end of the main corridor, just across from the principal's office, looking numbly at her reflection in the mirror. She still couldn't believe this was happening. In one sense it all felt so familiar, so incredibly familiar. She had been in that same bathroom a million times before, had checked her reflection the same way, smoothing her dark eyebrows, running a brush through her long, wavy hair. She knew Sweet Valley High as well as the back of her hand. Hadn't she suffered through years there? That morning, when she had walked through the main door, she had been overwhelmed with memories.

But in another sense she felt estranged. So much had happened since the day that she had walked out of Sweet Valley High supposedly for good. Her green eyes filled with tears, remembering: her mother's accident; the funeral; the long, numb days at work. First one job and then another, and none of them working out, until she ended up waitressing at the Whistle Stop, a café out on Route 1.

Johanna had been living a life that few of her classmates would be able to fathom. She had worked long, hard hours, had grown accustomed to earning money, to working with people much older than she was, many of them from backgrounds entirely different from her own. She sighed now, running the hairbrush automatically through her hair. It had been a far cry from the narrow, protected life-style she and Julie had always known.

It was funny how relative everything was. In school Johanna had always felt like the dummy, the one with bad grades, the one who couldn't keep up. But at the Whistle Stop everyone treated her with respect. The other waitresses always asked *her* how to spell things or to check a bill to see if it was added correctly. *They* hadn't thought of her as dumb, Johanna thought bitterly. But here—

Her thoughts were interrupted as the door to the bathroom burst open and two seniors, Yvonne White and Lisa Howard, came hurrying in. Both girls stopped short when they saw Johanna. They had all grown up in Sweet Valley and had been in many classes together, Until now, Johanna reminded herself. Now she was a year behind them.

"Johanna!" Lisa gasped in surprise. "What—I mean, are you—uh—"

"I'm coming back to school," Johanna said,

13

trying to sound calm, though her hands were shaking.

Yvonne's black eyes widened. "You're kidding," she said. "I thought you said you wouldn't come back no matter what!"

Fighting for control, Johanna took a deep breath. *Remember what you promised,* she told herself. *It isn't anyone's business but yours why you're coming back. Just stay cool and let them all think what they want.*

"I changed my mind," she said, trying to sound natural. "I just decided it would be a good idea to give it another try."

"Well!" Yvonne said brightly, taking out her makeup bag. "Are you going to have to repeat anything?"

"I'm going into the normal second-semester junior classes. They're going to get people to help me at first," Johanna said. She shuddered inwardly. *And, boy, am I going to need it,* she thought. School had always been hard for her, she would be coming into classes right in the middle of material she had never covered. It was going to be rough.

Making an awkward attempt at a lighthearted goodbye, Johanna excused herself and stepped out into the hallway. She could tell people were eyeing her curiously. People who knew her wondered why she was back, and people who didn't know her probably wondered who she was. Johanna swallowed nervously. She knew she looked good. She had taken extra special pains

14

with her appearance that morning, knowing she would need the confidence boost. Anyway, looks had never been Johanna's worry. She was an unusually pretty girl, and she knew it. Not that it made any difference. Everyone used to say she took after her mother, whereas Julie—round-faced, red-haired Julie—looked like their dad.

Johanna knew she was lucky to have inherited their mother's beauty. She had the same magnolia-white complexion, the same deep green eyes, the long, thick hair that tumbled almost to her waist in dark waves. But she would have traded it all in a second—less than a second—if she could be her sister Julie. Who cared if Julie wasn't gorgeous? She had what really mattered, talent. Julie was going to be a concert pianist. Everyone said so. She had been born with her parents' love of music, and when she played, it was, as their father had always said, like a little piece of heaven in advance.

It wasn't just talent that Julie had, though. She also had their father's love and respect. Johanna knew she herself could never win that, not when she was such an intellectual zero! Perhaps in another family Johanna's academic weakness wouldn't have been such a big deal. But in her family, intellectual things were all that mattered. Their father had a Ph.D. in music theory from UCLA. He taught music and played violin professionally. His hobby was philosophy, and his idea of relaxation was working a crossword puzzle or playing a difficult word game. Johanna had always felt left out. To make it worse, her mother and Julie seemed to share her father's tastes. Her mother—well, her mother had been just about perfect. When she wasn't singing she was reading—usually big Russian novels—which she insisted on reading in Russian. It just wasn't fair, Johanna thought. Here were these two geniuses, and they naturally expected to have genius children. On one count they did fine. Julie might not be a genius in school, but she was a genius when it came to the piano. Besides, she was just like them. She loved languages, philosophy, and having long, heated intellectual debates.

Johanna had always been different. It wasn't just that she bombed out in school, getting low scores on everything and feeling frustrated and miserable all the time. She just couldn't get excited about the things that excited the rest of her family. And it made her feel terrible. She couldn't help feeling that her father didn't love her as much as he loved Julie. And to tell the truth, she couldn't blame him.

Her mother, though, had managed to make Johanna feel incredibly loved, almost despite herself. Mrs. Porter used to take Johanna in her arms and whisper that one day she was going to find something of her own that she loved to do, and the whole world would look different. "It doesn't have to be music, sweetheart," she would say, stroking Johanna's long, dark hair. "Whatever it is, you just stick to it. Give it all you've got."

But Johanna hadn't found it. And she was less and less convinced she was going to get any closer to finding it at school.

By the middle of her junior year the frustration had become unbearable. After a period of doubts and indecision, Johanna had dropped out, insisting she was never going to go back. Her father had been devastated. Mrs. Porter, though she, too, believed it was a mistake, was more sympathetic. "Maybe you need some time off," she said softly. "Just promise me you won't close any doors behind you, sweetheart. Sometimes taking a stand can be more trouble than help. Don't be too rigid, not at your age."

Johanna continued to live at home, but every morning she went to work instead of school. It felt strange at first, but after a while she got used to it. She fell more or less into a new routine, and everything would have gone on in just that way if it hadn't been for the accident. After the accident none of them was ever the same again. It was as though a lightning bolt had struck, and the one person who mattered more than anyone else had vanished.

Mrs. Porter had been driving back late at night from a course she was teaching at the music academy in Los Angeles, and the roads were slippery from rain. The car that killed her was coming from the opposite direction. A young man was driving, a young man who had had too much to drink. He crossed the yellow line and drove straight into Mrs. Porter's car. She was killed instantly.

Instantly, Johanna thought now, swallowing back the tears. It had been more than six months since the accident, and all she had to do was think about it and she felt sick. One stupid second, and their mother was dead. The whole family seemed to fall apart, too, as if Mrs. Porter had been at the center of the wheel, holding the spokes in place, and once she was gone they all flew off in separate directions. Johanna knew how much her sister and father suffered during those long, dismal weeks after the accident, but she had never before felt so alienated from them. She knew her father and Julie were able to offer each other consolation, but neither could really talk to Johanna. Without her mother there to mediate, she felt that her connection to them both had vanished.

For months Johanna had tried to repress her mother's words of advice about not closing doors. She kept working, changing jobs when the boredom became too oppressive, trying not to think. She might have been stuck in that routine forever if she hadn't found her mother's journal. It had happened by accident. Johanna had been in the attic, looking for a photograph of her mother, which she wanted to frame and put in her room. She had found one, and she also found a cardboard box filled with things from her mother's bedroom, things Dr. Porter obviously hadn't been able to sort through and had simply put there for safekeeping. Johanna knew she was snooping, but she couldn't help herself. When she found the journal, she had been unable to put it down. Most of it was abstract and intellectual, musings on various subjects that Johanna didn't really understand. But then she came to a passage that she would never forget.

I would never say so to Johanna, because she needs to learn to trust herself. This is her own choice, and it must remain her own choice. But if it were up to me. . . . Those are painful words for a parent. I want her to go back to school so badly it makes me want to cry. What can I do? Do I owe it to her to speak my mind or to remain silent?

That was all. Sandwiched in the middle of long, rambling passages about other things, that tiny paragraph caused Johanna to slump down right where she was and sob as if her heart were breaking.

She never told her sister or father about the journal. She put it back where she had found it, and the next day she quit her job at the Whistle Stop and asked Dr. Porter if he would be willing to go with her to the principal and discuss the option of returning to school. Of course Dr. Porter and Julie wanted to know what had prompted her to return. Johanna had never told them. She felt her mother's journal was the last of many secrets she and her mother had shared.

Johanna knew her mother had kept silent about her decision out of love. How terribly hard it must have been for her not to say what she was dying to say—not to insist, not to plead, not to scold!

But her mother had loved her so much she had sacrificed her own feelings to allow Johanna the chance to make the decision truly her own.

Johanna didn't feel yet that she could determine whether or not it had been a mistake to drop out of school. But that didn't seem to be the point anymore. She had lost her mother's support at the time in her life when she needed it more than ever. To finish school—that was the last piece of advice her mother had been able to give her.

Johanna was bound and determined now to do it, however rough the battle was and however humiliated she felt.

Three

This should be getting easier, not harder, Johanna said to herself. She was waiting in the lunch line surrounded by other students, none of whom she knew very well. Some had moved to Sweet Valley during her absence, such as Regina Morrow, the stunning, raven-haired girl who had overcome deafness through a series of treatments in Switzerland. Some had changed radically, especially Regina's boyfriend, Bruce Patman, a senior and the only son of one of the richest families in the valley. In the old days he had been a real show-off, but since meeting Regina he had become much less arrogant. Bruce and Regina were so wrapped up in each other they didn't even seem to notice that Johanna was behind them. On the other side of her was a crowd of juniors—Caroline Pearce, a redhead whom Johanna barely knew; Robin Wilson, co-captain of the cheerleaders with Jessica Wakefield; Bill Chase, captain of the swim team, and his girlfriend DeeDee Gordon. Johanna sighed as she picked up a plastic tray from the pile and moved through the line. Nothing looked appetizing to her. The past few days had been rough, and it seemed as though her appetite had vanished.

Johanna had been placed in the easiest classes the board of education allowed. She was in second-year French, which was almost entirely filled with sophomores, and it was still murder for her. History, English, and government were all junior classes, but Johanna was finding them tough going, especially English. She read the stories Mr. Collins assigned, but she just couldn't see what she was supposed to get out of them. Like most of her classmates, she admired the handsome young teacher. With his strawberry-blond hair and blue eyes, he looked like a young Robert Redford. He was a great teacher, very relaxed and patient, yet he demanded a lot from his students. He had arranged for Johanna to work a few afternoons a week with Elizabeth Wakefield, one of the best students in her class. That afternoon Elizabeth was going to come over to the Porters' house and help Johanna with the F. Scott Fitzgerald short story she had been asked to write about. Johanna sighed. She hoped Elizabeth could help. For her own part, she was already frustrated to the point of tears.

Surprisingly, even algebra and chemistry were going badly. Johanna had always secretly loved math and science. But she couldn't seem to pay attention to the principles her teachers kept explaining. She felt bored, and she ended up letting her mind drift.

Johanna selected a carton of yogurt and some fruit at the end of the line, paid the cashier, and made her way into the crowded cafeteria, looking for a place to sit down. She found a quiet corner and was about to take a magazine out of her shoulder bag and pretend to absorb herself in it when she saw someone who made her stomach do a cartwheel.

It was Peter DeHaven.

For as long as she could remember, Johanna had had a crush on Peter. They had known each other since they were kids, and in grade school they used to spend hours playing with Peter's toy chemistry lab. Johanna admired him more than anyone she knew. Even when she was little, she knew there was something special about him. He was so smart—and so sure of himself! He could do anything.

As they got older, though, their friendship faded. Johanna's feelings didn't change, but Peter had less and less time for her as he threw himself into schoolwork. He was always polite when they spoke—he had sent a very kind note when he learned about her mother—but she could tell he wasn't interested in her. She bit her lip now, watching him sling his arm affectionately around Amy Sutton's shoulder. She couldn't help being surprised that he was dating someone like Amy. Amy was in one of

23

Johanna's classes and to her, the blond girl seemed silly and vain. She checked the disloyal thought at once. As far as Johanna was concerned, Peter DeHaven could do no wrong. If he was dating Amy, there must be something in her that Johanna just couldn't see.

"I'm going to buy some ice cream," Amy was saying to Peter, giving him a kiss before she left, as if she were leaving for a year instead of two minutes. Peter didn't seem to mind. He turned, caught sight of Johanna, and raised his eyebrows.

"Hey," he said, strolling over to her table. "What brings you back to Sweet Valley High?"

Johanna swallowed. She thought he was *so* cute. "I've decided to finish up," she said quietly.

Peter looked at her thoughtfully, fiddling with the change in his pocket. "That's great," he said at last. "You know, I missed you. This place just hasn't been the same without you around."

Johanna felt weak. "I—uh, I've missed you too," she mumbled. Only when *she* said it, the words didn't sound casual and flippant as they did when Peter said them. She was sure her feelings about him were written all over her face.

Are you taking any science courses?

Johanna blushed. "Chemistry," she said. Peter had taken chemistry when he was a *sophomore*. "I'm going to have to repeat some material, but it's probably for the best," she added inanely. God, what she would give to be able to make Peter respect her! Instead, he was smiling at her sympathetically.

"Nothing wrong with taking things slow," he said. "I'd be happy to help you with chemistry if you'd like. Just let me know."

Johanna was about to thank him when Amy came charging back from the lunch line, an ice-cream sandwich in her hand. "Peter," she said accusingly, staring pointedly at Johanna, "I thought you were going to find us someplace to *sit*!"

"Uh, I'll see you around, Johanna," Peter said.

Johanna nodded unhappily, watching Amy tuck her arm through his and steer him off toward a table crowded with people Johanna didn't know.

She felt horrible. It wasn't any use taking out her magazine and pretending to be interested in it. The truth was, she was in love with Peter. She had been for ages. Seeing him with his arm around another girl was just about more than she could stand!

"What do you think of this quiz?" Cara asked, lifting her sunglasses up to squint at Jessica and Elizabeth. The three girls were lying on striped towels on a sandy beach just a few miles from downtown Sweet Valley. Cara was reading aloud excerpts from the latest issue of *Ingenue* maga-

zine. " 'Is Your Relationship All It Could Be?' "
Cara read, putting her sunglasses on again.
"Hmmm," she said, studying the quiz.

Jessica groaned. "I *hate* that word," she
declared.

Elizabeth and Cara exchanged glances. "What
word?" Elizabeth asked.

"Relationship," Jessica said, making a face as
if she were eating something poisonous. "It's
so *boring*." She gave Cara a significant look.
"Especially for people our age," she pointed
out.

Cara giggled. "Something tells me I'm about
to get the famous Jessica Wakefield you're-too-
young-to-get-tied-down-to-someone lecture. Honestly, Jess, you're as bad as my mother sometimes!"

Jessica looked pained. She didn't want to act
like anyone's mother, but on the other hand,
maybe she had misjudged Mrs. Walker. "It's
bad enough doing everything with the same
guy when he's close by, like you and Jeffrey,"
she said magnanimously to her twin, who merely
rolled her eyes. "But, Cara, think about it! What's
the point in sticking with Steven when he isn't
even around half the time?"

Cara grinned. "I knew it," she said, throwing
the magazine down. "Come on, Jess. Let's hear
it. I know you're going to be miserable until
you've persuaded me, so go ahead and try."

Jessica sniffed. "I don't like your attitude,
Cara. Aren't I one of your very best friends?

Aren't I selflessly putting my feelings for you in front of my feelings for my own brother?"

Cara laughed. "I'm not persuaded yet," she said. "Maybe you should try that line about how my image will be destroyed if I don't go with someone new every week."

Jessica's eyes brightened. "That's right," she said. "People are going to think you're just waiting around for Steve because you can't do any better. I bet Steve thinks that himself."

A slight frown crossed Cara's face. "Steve would never think that," she said.

"Of course he wouldn't," Elizabeth assured her, picking up the magazine and thumbing through it.

"Don't bet on it," Jessica said darkly, sensing she had struck a sensitive area. "If I know Steve, it probably wouldn't hurt one little bit to make him realize there are other guys interested in you, too. For example," she added, her voice rising, "when was the last time he sent you a dozen roses?"

Cara blinked. "Uh—well, I guess never," she admitted. "Is that a bad sign?"

Jessica clapped her hand to her forehead. "Is that a bad sign?" she repeated. "Cara, are you kidding? He obviously doesn't even *respect* you. I bet if you agreed to go to the PTA dance with Ken Matthews, Steve would start sending you roses faster than you could say—"

"Jessica," Elizabeth cut in warningly.

"Right! Faster than you could say 'Jessica.' "
Jessica laughed.

Cara's brown eyes looked troubled. "I don't think you're right, Jess. Steve isn't the type. He hates gameplaying. And so do I," she added, trying to make her voice sound unconcerned.

But Cara was frowning. Jessica was sure she was getting somewhere, and as soon as Elizabeth took off for the Porters she could *really* get to work on her friend. Given this kind of a start, she was certain she could convince Cara to go out with other guys before Steven showed up on Friday.

She knew the two of them would thank her one day for making them see how crazy they'd been to try to tie each other down when they were both so young!

"Look," Elizabeth said, putting her hand on Johanna's arm. "Try not to panic. It's only a story! Just tell me what you thought about the main character. Did you feel sorry for him?"

Elizabeth was sitting next to Johanna at the big Formica table in the Porters' breakfast room. Julie was in the living room, practicing the piano, and Simone, the housekeeper, had gone upstairs to give them privacy.

But privacy didn't seem to be helping. Elizabeth took a deep breath and looked at Johanna, waiting for an answer. Johanna Porter really was a beautiful girl, she thought admiringly.

28

Her long hair made her look old-fashioned, and her eyes were such a beautiful shade of green. That afternoon Johanna was wearing a flowered jumper and a Victorian lace blouse. She had a style all her own, which Elizabeth thought was charming. But she couldn't help thinking what a shame it was that Johanna couldn't show the same independent style when it came to expressing her ideas. She seemed so unsure of herself.

"Oh, I don't know!" Johanna exclaimed at last, pushing the book away in despair. Her eyes filled with tears. "I can't even begin to say what I think about the story. I mean, it's just a story, isn't it? This man has a little girl, and he tries to get her back, only he can't. . . ."

"Do you sympathize with him?" Elizabeth asked. "Does he seem like he really loves the little girl, or not?"

Johanna looked distressed. "I guess he does love her. Yes, I *do* feel sorry for him." She sighed. "But that isn't really going to help me write an essay about him, is it?"

"Well, I think you have to start by figuring out what you think about it all," Elizabeth said. "One good place to start is to ask yourself what interests you most about the story." She picked up the anthology, turning to "Babylon Revisited."

"You could start with anything—the title, the style, the characterization—and just try to figure out how the author put it all together."

"OK," Johanna said, sighing heavily. "I'll try, Liz. Maybe by Friday I'll be a little more prepared to discuss things." She smiled sadly. "I guess I'm just finding it a little roughgoing right now."

Elizabeth squeezed her hand sympathetically. "I just want you to know that I think what you're doing is wonderful," she said earnestly. "You know you can call me anytime you need help, and it doesn't just have to be with English."

"Thanks," Johanna said, somewhat stiffly. "You're a big help, Liz. I really appreciate it."

Elizabeth sighed as she stood up and gathered her things together. She hoped Johanna was going to be able to make it. But from the way things looked right then, it wasn't going to be easy.

Four

It was Friday afternoon, and Johanna was working late by herself in the large chemistry lab at the end of the main corridor. Mr. Russo, her chemistry teacher, had given her a set of lab exercises to go through in order to catch up with the rest of the class. To her surprise, Johanna found herself enjoying the work. When she was left to work on her own, she found herself becoming absorbed in the experiments. That afternoon she was doing something simple, making sugar crystals. It was a lot of fun, and she was shocked when she looked up to discover that it was already four-thirty. She couldn't remember ever having lost track of time when she was doing schoolwork before!

Just then the door to the laboratory opened, and Peter walked in.

"Johanna!" he exclaimed, obviously as surprised to see her there as she was to see him. "What are you doing here on a Friday afternoon?"

Johanna explained that she was making up sections of the lab she had missed earlier that year. She could feel her face color as she spoke. Peter looked so cute, she thought. He was wearing a blue- and white-striped button-down shirt and khaki trousers, and with his short, dark hair and horn-rimmed glasses, he already looked like an East Coast college student. She blushed more deeply as Peter came closer to examine the results of her work.

"Sugar crystals!" Peter laughed and leaned over to look into the test tube she had set up on a stand. "I remember this book," he added, flipping through her lab book and smiling.

"What are *you* doing here so late?" Johanna asked him, feeling embarrassed about the elementary nature of her project.

Peter smiled. "I've been teaching a miniclass in chemistry over at the middle school this semester. It's really nothing special . . . just an enrichment session for gifted kids. Anyway, I'm teaching the last class next week, and I needed to pick up some materials."

Johanna looked at him with admiration. She couldn't believe he was *teaching* chemistry. "It's really nice of you to take the time to do that," she said softly. "I know how busy you must be with tennis and with college applications and everything. . . ."

"Well, tennis doesn't take up that much time," Peter assured her. "And I'm all set as far as college goes. I've been accepted early decision to MIT, and I've even set up a summer school course at Harvard beforehand so I can get a head start. I want to major in computer science," he told her. "I'm really interested in artificial intelligence and robotics, and I think an undergraduate degree in computer science is the best preparation."

Johanna stared at him. "You sound so— organized," she said. She couldn't even fathom having everything mapped out so carefully. He reminded her a little of her sister Julie, talking about studying music at Juilliard. Johanna blinked. For a brief instant she had a familiar, uncomfortable feeling of being locked out, of utter loneliness. How was it that other people seemed so certain of their plans and their interests? But as soon as Peter began talking about MIT, the feeling disappeared. After all, this wasn't music Peter was talking about. It was science. And Johanna always secretly had loved hearing about science.

For the next twenty minutes she listened attentively while Peter described in minute detail the program he would be studying. She heard about the dorm he wanted to be in at MIT, the physics professors whose work he most admired, the special artificial intelligence programs he hoped to get involved with. She could hardly believe this was the same Peter DeHaven she had known since she was little. It was so much fun to listen to him, to see someone her age who knew exactly what he wanted from life, and who was so certain he would be able to attain it!

Johanna couldn't resist trying to put some of these feelings into words. "I'm really excited for you," she said sincerely. "I think you're perfect for MIT, Peter. You're going to do well there. And the thing is, you'll really take advantage of all the opportunities you come across. I mean, how many other guys are going to have bothered to find out what professors they want to work with, even before they start freshman year?"

Peter smiled. "Well, you have to go for things, Johanna," he said matter-of-factly. "It's pretty cutthroat out there. You can't just sit back and watch it all go past you."

Johanna swallowed. *Which is exactly what I've been doing,* she thought sadly. *Just sitting by and watching life go past.* But what if you didn't know what you wanted? What if—

Her reflections were interrupted as Peter launched into a description of the computer program he was trying to enter in the Southern California Science Fair. "I want to write one of those programs that acts like a psychologist— you know, that asks various questions about feelings, fears, that sort of thing. I've been reading all the books on computer programming I can get my hands on, and I think I've got a pretty good idea how to go about it."

Johanna was impressed. The more she listened to Peter the more she admired him. He

34

was without a doubt the most confident, self-assured guy she had ever known. He didn't seem to have the slightest doubt about anything he said or did.

"Hey," Peter said suddenly, looking at her closely. "Have you got plans for this weekend?"

Johanna was so astonished she almost fell off her laboratory stool. "Uh—no, not really," she said. Not really! *That* was the understatement of the year, she thought.

"I was just thinking. Maybe you'd like to drive out to Las Palmas Canyon with me tonight. A friend of my older brother's lives near there, and I'm supposed to drive by and get some of his notes. He's a computer jock, and I think he can help me out a little. If you feel like it, I'd love the company."

Johanna pulled her hair back from her neck with both hands. Las Palmas Canyon was about twenty miles from Sweet Valley, a breathtaking gorge that had always been one of her favorite places. She could hardly believe Peter was asking her to accompany him. What about Amy? she thought. But she was afraid to ask.

"I'd love to go with you," she said happily.

"Great. I'll pick you up around seven-thirty. How's that?"

"That's fine," Johanna said. She still couldn't believe this had actually happened. She was going out with Peter DeHaven, and on a Friday night, too!

Johanna was so excited that she squelched

the warning voice inside her, which was trying to remind her that if Peter hadn't run into her in the lab, he would have just gone off to the canyon without her.

And he hadn't asked her anything about herself. He had been so busy describing his own plans that he hadn't asked a single thing about her.

But she excused his behavior as she cleaned up her lab materials. They were old friends, after all. And who could blame Peter for being more interested in his own plans than in hers? For heaven's sake, she thought. It wasn't as if she even *had* any plans. There was no doubt about it. Peter's life was a million times more interesting than hers.

And if *she* felt that way, why shouldn't he?

"Hi!" Johanna called as she opened the front door of her house. She could hear the sound of scales from the living room. Julie was practicing, and apparently Simone had gone home. Dr. Porter was in San Francisco for four days, and the house had the peculiar empty quality that seemed to settle over it whenever he was gone. But it always felt empty now, Johanna thought sadly. Without her mother, it always would.

She straightened, reminding herself about Peter and their plans for that evening. Resolving not to get depressed, she hurried into the living room and threw herself into the armchair next to the piano. She listened while Julie worked out a particularly complicated set of scales.

"Hey," Julie said, turning to her with a smile. "Congratulations on making it through your first week back!"

"Thanks," Johanna said, grinning. "You know," she added thoughtfully. "It really wasn't *that* bad." Soon she was filling Julie in on all the events of that day, including her meeting with Peter in the lab.

"He's so cute," she concluded with a sigh.

"Yeah." Julie smiled, "You've always had kind of a thing for him, haven't you?" She turned back to her sheet music. "But I guess he's pretty absorbed these days, isn't he?"

"What do you mean?" Johanna asked, wondering whether or not this was the best time to tell her sister about her plans to accompany Peter to Las Palmas Canyon.

"Oh, I don't know. I like Peter, but he really seems awfully sold on himself since he found out he got into MIT. I think his ego's getting a little too big," Julie remarked. "Amy seems to be the only person he listens to."

Johanna flushed and ignored the comment about Amy. "*I* think he's really nice," she objected. "OK, so he's excited about MIT. But who wouldn't be?"

Julie shrugged. "Yeah, I guess so," she said.

"Actually," Johanna said, fiddling with the edge of her spiral notebook, "I'm going out with him tonight. We're going to drive out to Las Palmas. He has a friend out there he wants to visit."

Julie's eyes widened. "I don't know if that's such a great idea. After all, Peter is going out with Amy Sutton."

"Well, that didn't seem to bother him," Johanna said defensively. "So why should it bother me?"

Julie's brow wrinkled. "It seems a little coincidental," she pointed out, "that Amy just *happens* to be going up to the mountains with her parents this weekend. Did Peter mention that?"

Johanna paled. "I don't see what the big deal is!" she cried, jumping to her feet. As a matter of fact, Peter *hadn't* mentioned it. And it bothered her to think that she had been invited only because Amy was unavailable and wouldn't be around to object.

But she wasn't going to let Julie see how upset she was about Amy Sutton. "You're just trying to make me feel lousy," she snapped. "Isn't it possible that Peter asked me to go with him because he *likes* me?"

Julie's eyes were troubled. "Of course it's possible! He'd be a fool if he didn't, Jo. Don't get mad at me," she pleaded. "I'm just afraid you'll get hurt. I mean, Peter's a nice guy and everything, but all he seems to care about lately is Peter!"

"You don't even know him," Johanna said

accusingly. "You just think he's egotistical because he cares about science, and not music!"

"Johanna, that isn't fair," Julie protested, her voice quavering.

But Johanna didn't care. She felt as if everything were crumbling. She had come home in a wonderful mood, looking forward to the evening. And, as usual, all it took was opening the front door for everything to change.

She couldn't believe now that she had actually been foolish enough to hope, for once, that she could share something with her sister. It was just impossible, and that was all there was to it.

But Johanna was certain of one thing: She wasn't going to let Julie spoil her excitement about Peter. He was the first good thing that had happened to her since their mother had died. And nothing Julie said or did was going to change how excited she felt that he had noticed her at last!

Five

"So, how's my favorite pair of clones?" Steven Wakefield asked with a mischievous smile, his dark eyes twinkling as he entered the kitchen.

"Steven!" Elizabeth shouted. She engulfed her brother in a hug. It was late Friday afternoon, and the twins had been waiting anxiously for their brother to arrive.

"Hey, ugly," Steven said, rumpling Jessica's hair and laughing when she made a face. Steven loved to tease Jessica about her appearance, and his long-standing jokes about her looks never failed to bother her.

"You're not looking so hot yourself," Jessica muttered, wriggling away from him. Elizabeth and Steven laughed at how irate she sounded. In truth, Steven Wakefield was an extremely good-looking young man. He had thick, dark hair, brown eyes that crinkled up at the corners when he smiled, and a broad, athletic build.

"I don't suppose I can convince either of you

two to help me lug some of my stuff inside," Steven added, looking through the kitchen door at his yellow Volkswagen.

"We'd be glad to. Wouldn't we, Jess?" Elizabeth said pointedly before her twin could manufacture an excuse to disappear. The three of them walked outside, and Steven started taking bags out of the trunk.

Jessica picked up the smallest bag, then groaned under the weight of it. "What have you got in here? Rocks?" She grumbled.

"Just clothes and shoes and things. A few presents for Cara," Steven said nonchalantly. "We have an anniversary coming up, you know."

"Well, *that's* hardly a surprise, considering you guys celebrate practically every *week* since you met," Jessica muttered.

Elizabeth gave her brother a smile. "I think that's really sweet, Steve. I'm sure Cara will be so happy." She picked up a large laundry bag and took it inside, leaving Steven and Jessica alone outside.

"It's funny," Jessica said, thinking fast. "I don't seem to remember Cara mentioning anything about an anniversary. I guess she's just been so busy lately she kind of forgot about it."

Steven glanced at her. "Busy? What do you mean?"

"Oh . . . nothing," Jessica said airily, waving her hand dismissively and adjusting the bag over her shoulder. "I mean, nothing *important*," she corrected herself.

Steven studied her closely and then shrugged, but Jessica wasn't through with him. "You know how it is," she said as they entered the house. "You go to a party here, another party there. Before you know it, you've barely even got time to think! Let alone," she said, panting and shifting the bag, "time to remember something like an *anniversary*."

Steven cleared his throat as they walked through the house to the stairs. "I didn't know Cara was going out so much," he said casually.

Jessica's voice shot up an octave. "Really?" she demanded. "You're *kidding*!" Somehow Jessica managed to inject as much significance into this oversight as was possible. "I'm sure it doesn't mean anything—her keeping it quiet, I mean," she added.

Steven laughed. "I'm sure it doesn't," he said, setting his bags down at the top of the stairs.

"Of course it *could* mean she didn't, you know, want you to know," Jessica added as if that explanation had just occurred to her. "But I'm sure that couldn't possibly be true. At least, from the impression *I* got—"

"Jess," Steven said, his patience wearing thin, "are you trying to tell me something? Because if you are, I think we're having a communication gap. I haven't got the slightest idea what you're talking about."

"Steve? I put the bag in your room, OK?" Elizabeth called.

Jessica followed her brother into his bedroom, glad Elizabeth was heading down the hall to her own room, where she would be safely out of earshot. "What are you guys doing tonight?" she asked innocently.

"I'm taking Cara out to dinner. There's a new French place I want to take her to, Maison Blanche, that's supposed to be really great. Jason took Betsy there, and he said it's incredibly romantic."

Jessica picked up a framed photograph of Cara from her brother's desk, inspected it, and set it down again. "I bet it'll be nice for you two to be together again," she said thoughtfully. "I mean, it must be so *hard* having to deal with all these separations. And then the stress of dating other people . . ."

Steven looked at her. "Who dates other people?" he asked mildly. "I don't. And as far as I know, Cara doesn't either."

Jessica laughed.

"Jessica," Steven said, looking annoyed, "Is there something going on that I should know about, or are you just losing your mind?"

Jessica's eyebrows shot up. "I'm sure Cara wouldn't even *consider* them dates," she said. "It's just that I know she's got some good friends who happen to be guys, that's all. It's not a big deal," she added, making it sound as if Steven were the one who was being suspicious. "For heaven's sake, Steve, you can't expect the poor girl to sit around *knitting* or something while you're off at college having a great time!"

"I never said I expected that!" Steven snapped. "As far as I'm concerned, she's perfectly free to do whatever she wants to do." He looked distressed. "I guess I just hoped she wouldn't *want* to go out with other guys, that's all."

"That's OK, Steven," Jessica said gently, patting him on the shoulder. "It's hard not to be possessive. You can't help it."

With that, she left the room, certain she had left him so muddled he had no idea what to think!

Johanna had taken unusual pains with her appearance on Friday evening, and by the time Peter came by for her she knew she looked wonderful. She was wearing a blue cotton, flower-print Laura Ashley dress, and her long hair hung loose around her shoulders. She didn't wear makeup. Her eyelashes were so dark she didn't need mascara, and her complexion was beautiful. But she did dab on a little perfume. Peter whistled when he saw her.

"You look like you belong out in a meadow somewhere," he said, backing off and looking her up and down appreciatively. He took her hand and walked her over to his car, a navy blue Mazda. His fingers felt warm and strong around hers.

"I really appreciate your coming out to Las Palmas with me," he told her as he opened the door for her. Johanna's eyes closed briefly. She couldn't help noticing the scent of soap as Peter leaned, just for a second, against her. Her stomach did a sudden flip-flop.

"It's a beautiful night," she murmured. It was, too. As usual, the temperature had dropped so that it was cool enough to require a light sweater. The evening air was slightly humid and smelled of lush Southern California flowers. There was a new moon out. The canyon would be beautiful.

Peter started the car, and as they drove he asked, "What kind of music do you like?" He turned on the radio.

Johanna laughed. Funny question to ask a Porter, she thought. Peter obviously didn't see the joke, and he didn't press it. He just selected a station himself.

"I'm really looking forward to meeting this guy," he said instead. "I think he'll be able to help me with this program. Johanna, I can't tell you how badly I want to win this science fair."

Johanna shifted in the seat. "Is there a big prize?" she asked.

Peter nodded. "It's not even the prize, though. It's the honor. I've looked forward to entering this contest since I was about ten. It's only for high school seniors, though, so it's a one-shot deal. And the prize is nice, too," he added.

"They give the first-prize winner a scholarship to use at the college of his choice."

"Or *her* choice," Johanna said suddenly.

Peter stared at her, then turned back to look at the road. "Yes," he said. "Or *her* choice." He was quiet for a minute. "You don't seem like the sort," he added strangely.

"What sort?" Johanna asked him.

"You know, the sort who cares about using 'his' instead of 'his and hers.' That sort of thing." Peter looked uneasy, as if he were on unsteady ground.

Johanna bit her lip. She was thinking how strange it was for Peter to decide what "sort" she was at all, when he had never asked her a single thing about herself. But she didn't want to argue with him. She liked him, despite the fact that he was undeniably wrapped up in himself.

"Tell me more about your computer program," she said, settling back in the seat.

Peter relaxed considerably. "Promise you'll tell me if I start going on and on about it, though," he instructed. "I know I can get kind of carried away."

For the next twenty minutes, Peter explained his idea to her. Johanna thought it sounded intriguing. And she was impressed that Peter would have come up with a program that so clearly demonstrated an interest in inner feelings. She knew some science students tended to forget the emotional side of things in their efforts to learn facts, to memorize, to reduce things to formulae. Peter clearly wasn't like that. She thought the plan to make a program that could ask—and help "solve"—certain simple questions about the subject's emotional life was a superb one. And she enjoyed hearing about the process he planned to use to write the program. In fact, she was surprised that it made so much sense to her. But then he was simplifying everything for her benefit, she thought. She would probably never get it on her own.

In no time, it seemed, they had reached Peter's brother's friend's house. Larry Mills was in his early twenties and had already landed a job at a major computer manufacturer. He was a relaxed, likeable guy who made Johanna feel instantly at ease. To her surprise, he seemed interested in her, asking her dozens of questions about herself, her family, her hobbies. She couldn't tell how closely Peter was following the conversation, though. He seemed to be deep in thought. At last Larry turned to him and began to talk about computers and computer programming, and it was Johanna's turn to tune out. She was tired, she realized suddenly. It had been a long week, and she was grateful when Peter said he was ready to go.

"Let's drive to the canyon and see what it looks like tonight," he suggested as they got back in the car. "It doesn't seem fair to drag you all the way out here just to sit in Larry's living room."

"I didn't mind at all. But it would be fun to drive out to the canyon," Johanna said quickly. She shivered a little in anticipation. It was such a beautiful night!

"Cold?" Peter said, putting his right arm around her and pulling her over against him.

Johanna swallowed. Her leg was touching his. "No. I just had a chill for a second," she whispered.

It was only a five-minute drive from Larry's house to the canyon. Johanna's breath caught as she saw the beautiful gorge before them. "I just love this place," she murmured, staring out at the stark terrain. "It looks—I don't know—so desolate and so beautiful at the same time. Doesn't it?"

"Johanna," Peter said softly. He still had his arm around her, but he had turned the engine off and was staring straight ahead at the canyon. She liked hearing him say her name. "I'm glad I brought you out here," he added, turning to face her.

Johanna took a deep breath. His face looked so intense—as if she were a puzzle he were trying to solve.

"Can I—" He reached over and stroked her cheek, his hand surprisingly gentle. "Johanna, can I kiss you?"

Johanna didn't answer. Her eyes closed almost automatically as he leaned forward, his lips brushing hers. The next thing she knew he was clasping her tightly in his arms, murmuring her name over and over against her ear. She felt that she never wanted him to let go of her again. Everything else seemed to fall away, the pain of missing her mother, the worries about school, the anxiety over her argument with Julie. All that mattered was Peter and what was happening then.

Six

On Sunday afternoon Johanna went over to the Wakefields' house for another tutorial session with Elizabeth. It was a beautiful, sunny day, and the girls set their things up on one of the small white patio tables near the Wakefields' swimming pool so they could enjoy the sunshine while they worked. Elizabeth kept thinking that Johanna looked different that afternoon, though she couldn't say why. As always she was startlingly pretty. That day she was wearing a flowered cotton skirt and a soft, Victorian-looking white blouse. Was it that her expression was softer somehow? Elizabeth wasn't sure. But Johanna seemed friendlier, more receptive, more eager to talk.

They had moved on to the next story in the anthology, one about a young man and woman who were desperately in love. "It's funny how so much literature seems to be about love,"

Johanna said thoughtfully, twisting a lock of dark hair around one finger.

Elizabeth looked at her with a smile. "Well, I guess it's one of the most basic emotions," she said. "Writers try to capture universal experiences. And what could be more universal than falling in love?"

Johanna blushed. "I guess you're right," she murmured, dropping her gaze.

Elizabeth was almost certain that Johanna was making an effort to confide in her, so she risked an intrusive question. "Johanna, are you interested in anyone special? I was wondering whether or not you met anyone when you were working?"

Johanna laughed. "You should've seen the guys at the Whistle Stop," she said. "If you had, you'd never have thought that." She was quiet for a minute. "But actually, now that you mention it. . . . Liz, I know we're supposed to be concentrating on analyzing short stories, but would you mind if I asked your advice about something? I have a feeling you're really objective about this sort of thing."

"You can certainly ask my advice," Elizabeth assured her. "And I'll try my hardest to be objective."

Johanna took a deep breath. "You see, I've told my sister Julie all about it, but she thinks I'm nuts. She thinks Peter's just using me or something."

"Peter?" Elizabeth repeated blankly.

"Peter DeHaven," Johanna said with a sigh. "I know it's ridiculous. I mean, here he is, probably the smartest person in the school. And I'm probably the dumbest." She shook her head, her long, dark hair tumbling over her shoulders. "But I can't help it, Liz. I've had this awful crush on him ever since I can remember. And now that I'm back in school I feel like—I don't know. It must sound so silly to you, but every time I see him I get these incredible butterflies in my stomach. Do you think I'm being a flake?"

Elizabeth looked seriously at her. "I certainly don't blame you for having a crush on Peter," she said carefully. "I always had the impression you two were pretty good friends. Is that still true?"

"Well, I think we're more than just friends now," Johanna said. "Promise you won't tell a soul, Liz. We went out together Friday night, and I had the most fantastic time."

Elizabeth's eyebrows shot up. "I thought—I mean, I don't want to say anything I shouldn't, but I thought he was going out with Amy Sutton."

"Oh, he has been," Johanna said hastily, "but I don't think it's very serious. In fact, I'm almost positive he's going to break up with her as soon as she gets back from the mountains with her family."

"Oh, she was away this weekend," Elizabeth

said. She didn't think the situation sounded very promising. If it were anyone but Peter DeHaven—but Elizabeth couldn't help feeling as if Peter's main interest was *Peter*. He seemed wrapped up in himself and his own affairs. She hoped he wasn't leading Johanna on. The girl seemed so vulnerable.

"Yes, and my sister seems to think Peter asked me out just because Amy was away. But I'm sure it's more than that. I just wondered if you think it would be wrong for me to go over and visit him this afternoon, just to sort of say hello. Maybe he could help me with my chemistry, too."

"Well, I really don't know Peter well at all," Elizabeth said slowly. "I mean, he *seems* really nice and everything, and I'm sure—" She hesitated. "I just don't know, Johanna. I guess I'd have to say just to go ahead and do whatever feels right."

Johanna smiled. "I think I *will* drop by, then," she decided. "I'm sure Julie's wrong, Elizabeth. Peter's absolutely fantastic! I know he'd never hurt anyone deliberately." Her eyes shining, she began to describe the project Peter was working on for the science fair. Suddenly the patio door opened, and Steven came out, a stormy expression on his handsome face.

"I hope one of you two is an ace mathematician," he grumbled. "Otherwise, I think I'm cooked!"

Elizabeth couldn't help giggling. She knew

Steven had some problem sets to work on that week, and math had never been his favorite subject.

"Steve, this is Johanna Porter," she said, still smiling. "Johanna, my brother Steve."

"Your very *grouchy* brother Steve," Steven amended, plopping down next to Elizabeth and throwing a manila folder on the table. "Why is it my whole life seems to have collapsed in the space of twenty-four hours?"

Elizabeth raised her eyebrows. "Sounds serious," she said, closing her anthology. It appeared as though English literature was going to have to wait for a while.

"Women," Steven said heavily, raising both hands in a gesture of helplessness. "I'm telling you, there's nothing worse in the whole world than trying to figure out what you've done wrong when you know you haven't done *anything*!"

"I take it you and Cara have had a fight," Elizabeth said with a sympathetic smile.

"Yeah," Steven said miserably. "But I can't figure out why. All of a sudden she just started getting furious with me, asking me all these questions about girls at school, acting like I don't care about her just because she lives here and I'm an hour away." He shook his head and sighed. "What a mess. And to make everything worse, I've got this ridiculous set of math problems to do, and I can't even begin to figure them out."

He pulled a sheet out of his manila envelope. "Look at these things!" he cried, holding them up for Johanna and Elizabeth's inspection. "They're called 'spatial relationships' or something equally incomprehensible." He shuddered. "Give me a short story any day!"

Johanna looked at the sheet with interest. "Oh I used to have a puzzle book filled with this sort of thing." She smiled. "I always thought they were kind of fun."

Steven stared at her. The exercises consisted of a series of boxes that were unfolded; and in each the problem was to determine what shape the box would be when it was folded. "But don't you need to have taken advanced math to be able to do these?" he asked.

Johanna shrugged. "I don't know. I just always did them for fun. Look," she added, taking out a pencil. "All you do is measure the angles. You can do it mentally, so you don't really have to figure it out. Then you can determine what the folded shape will look like." She whizzed through the problems in minutes while Elizabeth and Steven looked on in amazement.

"Johanna, have you ever told Ms. Taylor about this little knack of yours?" Elizabeth asked.

Johanna laughed. "Why should I? It doesn't seem to help much when it comes to algebra tests."

Steven looked thoughtfully at her. "Maybe you're bored," he said. "I bet if you were in a more challenging math class you'd blow everyone away."

Johanna blushed. "It's nothing! I've just always liked that kind of puzzle. I like, you know, having concrete problems to work out. It feels really satisfying when you get them right."

"Well, the next time I've got a set of problems to work out, I know who I'm going to turn to!" Steven declared.

Johanna made a dismissive gesture with her hand, but Elizabeth could tell the girl was pleased.

In fact Johanna's pleasure was evident even after Steven had disappeared inside to call Cara and try to make amends. It was obvious that helping Steven had boosted Johanna's confidence. Her face glowed, and when they turned back to the story they had been reading, Johanna seemed much more willing to volunteer opinions about the characters.

"The problem with literature," she admitted, "is that there doesn't seem to be any way to *solve* it. Do you know what I mean? There doesn't seem to be a right answer or a wrong answer."

"That's true," Elizabeth agreed. "But I guess that's part of what makes it fun. You find yourself making all sorts of connections between what happens to the characters in the story and what's happening in your own life. Things may not be 'right' or 'wrong,' but you can still learn a lot from them."

"Boy, I hope I don't find too many connections between this story and my own life." Johanna giggled. The story was about a tragic love affair, and Elizabeth laughed along with her.

But she couldn't help remembering what Johanna had confided to her about Peter DeHaven. Elizabeth knew it wasn't any of her business, and even though Johanna had asked for advice, she felt it wasn't her place to interfere.

Still, she couldn't help feeling that Peter was bad news. And she, too, hoped that their friendship didn't come to resemble the unhappy love affair in the story they had been studying.

Jessica and Cara were at the Box Tree Café in town, having some iced tea before the game of doubles tennis they had lined up with Bruce Patman and his cousin Roger. The Patmans, who lived in one of the luxurious mansions on the hill overlooking the valley, had their own grass courts, and Cara and Jessica loved playing there. Jessica made a mental note to report back to Steven that Cara had been *especially* excited about playing with Bruce. Granted, both Bruce and Roger had steady girlfriends. But with a little insinuation, Jessica could make it seem as if Cara were just a tiny bit interested in Bruce.

"I don't understand how we ended up getting in another stupid argument," Cara said now with a sigh, taking a sip of her iced tea and looking disconsolately at Jessica. "It just all came out of nowhere, and we'd just finished making up! He kept asking if I felt tied down, and I kept saying I didn't, and then I started getting suspicious, wondering whether he didn't just *want* me to say I felt tied down because *he* feels tied down. And the next thing I knew we were furious with each other again!"

"I told you that long-distance love leads to nothing but problems," Jessica told her. "I wouldn't worry about it," she added a moment later. "I'm sure Steve will come crawling back in no time."

"So you don't think I should call and apologize? I really think *I* was the one who was being totally irrational," Cara said.

"Never!" Jessica gasped, horrified. "Cara, do you want him to start taking you for granted? Just assuming he can treat you like dirt and walk all over you and you'll still come back to him?"

"He didn't—"

"And besides," Jessica added, looking grim, "*I* happen to think Steve needs to realize that you're willing to stand up to him. Maybe once he sees that, he'll stop seeing all these women up at school."

"What women?" Cara asked, her face draining of color.

"Oh," Jessica said airily, "no one special. You know how it is. A little dance here, a movie there—

"He never told me he was going out with anyone!" Cara wailed.

"Cara, of course he didn't," Jessica hissed. He hadn't told *Jessica* he was going out with anyone other than Cara, either. But Jessica was sure he must be. And even if he wasn't, it was all part of the plan to help Cara and Steven gain some independence. "He wants to keep you dangling on a string," Jessica told her friend. "That way, whenever he drops into town, you'll be ready and waiting for him. Wise up," she admonished. "If you keep this up, Cara, he'll just completely lose respect for you. It's much better to get out while you've still got some tiny little bit of self-respect left."

Cara seemed ready to cry. "That rotten creep," she muttered. "If I'd had any idea he was seeing girls up at school . . . and the whole time I've been turning dates down right and left!"

"I told you," Jessica said with obvious satisfaction. "What could possibly be more stupid than turning down a date? Unless it's with someone horrible," she added.

Cara was barely listening. From the expression on her face, it was obvious that she was upset. But Jessica knew that in the long run Cara would be much better off without Steven, and Steven would be much better off without her.

It wouldn't be long before they would both thank her for saving them from making a complete mess of their lives!

"How was your tennis game?" Elizabeth asked her twin, coming into Jessica's bedroom and clearing a small space on her chair so she could sit down.

Jessica was concentrating hard on the new set of nightly exercises she had copied down from that month's issue of *Ingenue*. "It was OK," she mumbled, bouncing her head down to touch her knee. She tossed her blond hair back as she sat up again. "We lost, of course. But then what do you expect? Bruce Patman isn't gentlemanly enough to throw a game."

Elizabeth looked thoughtfully at her twin. "Can I ask you a question?"

Jessica giggled. "Nope. No questions tonight, Liz. I can't think and keep my thighs in shape at the same time."

Elizabeth grinned. "I'm serious, Jess. Do you think Amy and Peter DeHaven are going to keep seeing each other?"

"Who knows? Amy's acting really weird ever since they started going out." Jessica frowned. "I think she may have gotten in over her head. I mean, she's really obsessed with him. She calls him all the time, and he's all she ever talks about anymore. It's kind of boring."

Elizabeth wasn't in the mood to hear Jessica's opinions on steady dating. She was thinking about Johanna. "So he really matters to Amy," she mused.

"Why the sudden interest in Amy Sutton? I thought you'd decided she was too flaky for you these days."

Elizabeth's brow was furrowed. "If I tell you why, do you swear not to tell a single soul?"

Jessica's blue-green eyes widened. "Of course!" she said solemnly.

"No, I mean it, Jess," Elizabeth said warningly. "If you tell Amy—or Lila—or Cara—or *anyone* that I told you, I'll never speak to you again as long as I live!"

"I promise!" Jessica cried, one hundred percent of her attention focused now on her twin. "Come on. What's up?"

"Well, apparently Peter asked Johanna Porter out Friday night," Elizabeth said with a sigh. "I'm really worried about it, too. Johanna seems so vulnerable right now. She says she's always had kind of a crush on him, and it sounds like he might be taking advantage of that."

Jessica's eyebrows shot up. "You mean he asked Johanna out while Amy was away this weekend?" She looked horrified. "What a creep! Amy would absolutely *die* if she ever found out."

"Well, she isn't going to," Elizabeth said grimly, getting up from the chair. "At least not from either one of us. You promised, remember?"

"I remember," Jessica said. "Don't worry," she added, seeing the suspicious look on her twin's face. "Amy's one of my closest friends. I

61

wouldn't hurt her feelings for anything in the world."

"Good," Elizabeth said. She sighed again, her expression unhappy. "I don't want to see Amy get hurt either. But I'm much more concerned about Johanna, to tell you the truth. I'm really afraid that Peter will hurt Johanna—and in her state it could be devastating."

Jessica nodded. "I hate to say so, Liz, "but I have a terrible feeling you're right."

Seven

Johanna took special pains with her appearance Monday. She kept telling herself not to expect too much, but she knew she would see Peter at school, and she wanted to look her best. It seemed pointless not to be excited. After all, when she had dropped by his house the day before, he had been happy to see her. Emboldened by her talk with Elizabeth, Johanna had broached the subject of Amy. He hadn't made any direct promises, but she had gotten the impression that things weren't serious between them, that he had been considering ending the relationship, and planning to talk to her when she got back from the mountains.

So Johanna didn't think she was being unrealistic to daydream a little about the future with Peter. In homeroom everyone was talking about the big PTA dance, which was going to be held that Friday night, and she wondered whether Peter had already asked Amy. Even if he had, they wouldn't still go together if they broke up this week, would they? And if Peter was free, wouldn't he want to take Johanna? She knew exactly what she'd wear, too, her spaghetti-strap sun dress with the gold-and-rose-colored flowers. It was perfect, just bare enough, but not *too* bare. She was so absorbed in her day-dream that she barely noticed when the home-room bell rang. Lucy Hawkins, a thin girl with mousy brown hair, who had always been slightly mean to Johanna, came up behind her and laughed.

"I bet she can't even pass *homeroom*," Johanna heard Lucy say to her friend Carol Ulrich.

Johanna's face turned bright red, but she held her head high as she slid out of her seat. Who cared what Lucy Hawkins thought? Elizabeth and Steven thought she was doing fine. And so did Peter. With an indifferent expression on her face, she sailed past Lucy, vowing not to show she cared. She was going to make it. Not just for her mother, but for Peter, too. She was going to show him she was smart as well as pretty. She was going to make him proud of her!

The hall was crowded between classes, and Johanna had to steel herself before navigating her way from homeroom to her first-period English class. She had to pass the student lounge, and her pulse quickened when she saw the familiar dark head above the crowd. It was Peter, standing with his back to her, talking to a group of people—Amy Sutton, Lila Fowler, Jessica Wakefield, Ken Matthews, and Aaron Dallas. Johanna took a deep breath. The group was standing outside the door to the lounge, and she had to walk past them to get to Mr. Collins's room.

I'm not going to be a coward this time, she told herself sharply. *I'm going to say hello!* Her stomach did a flip as she got closer. Amy Sutton saw her coming and apparently said something, and the whole group laughed. Johanna bit her lip.

"Peter," Johanna said, stopping short and putting her hand on his arm, "how are things?" She tried hard to sound casual and matter-of-fact, but she could tell her face was red. The whole group stared, first at her and then at Peter. Clearly everyone was waiting for his response.

Peter looked at her without a smile. "Oh, hi," he said tersely. Then he turned back to face the others. Without saying another word, Johanna felt as if she had been slapped. She could barely believe what had happened. How could he snub her like that? Especially after the weekend! She walked away, Amy's laughter burning her ears, her eyes filling with tears. *What an idiot*, she told herself. *What a giant-size complete, total fool.* How could she possibly have kidded herself into believing Peter would ever care about her? Obviously Julie had been right. He had been willing to spend some time with her over the weekend, when Amy was out of town. Now that she was back, all he cared about was being with his cool friends. They all thought Johanna was a joke, and obviously so did he.

Hot tears burned her eyes, but Johanna refused to lose control and cry at school. She was going to get through the day somehow, but that was it. She didn't ever want to go back. It was too humiliating. She had been a fool to think she could make it.

Johanna spent her lunch hour that day working in the chemistry lab. Dispirited as she was, it made her feel better to do something constructive. And she was enjoying chemistry. *I shouldn't give up now*, she told herself, pouring a solution into a test tube. *Not now, when I'm just starting to make progress*. Just then the door to the lab opened, and Peter came in.

"I was hoping I'd find you in here," he said. "Johanna, I'm really sorry about this morning. I felt really awkward in front of Amy and her friends, and I guess I made a mess of things. I just hope you'll forgive me."

Johanna blinked. That was the last thing she had expected, and she was so surprised to see him at all she barely knew what to say. Peter didn't seem to mind. He seemed perfectly happy to do all the talking.

"The thing is, I'm so afraid of hurting Amy," he began, sitting down beside Johanna and looking at her, a serious expression in his dark eyes.

"She really seems to have a thing for me. I feel that I've got to let her down easy, you know what I mean?"

Johanna swallowed. "But you're still planning on splitting up with her?"

"I definitely am," Peter assured her. "I just want to do it gradually. In fact I'm planning on talking to her tonight. I'd promised to go over to her house for dinner, and afterwards— well, I'm going to let her know things have changed." He leaned over and took Johanna's hands in his. "I hope I haven't messed anything up between us," he said gently.

Johanna blushed. His hands felt so warm around hers. It was just so hard to figure out what to do! He looked so sincere. The expression in his eyes made her melt. But at the same time . . . "You really hurt my feelings, the way you brushed me off this morning," she blurted out. "I felt like I wasn't important enough even to say hello to. I felt terrible."

Peter's eyes were filled with concern. "I'm so sorry," he said. "Johanna, promise me you'll give me a chance to make it up to you. Can I take you out to dinner tomorrow night? Just the two of us? I know a wonderful place in Bridgewater, about fifteen miles from here. It's really special. I'd love it if you'd let me take you there."

Johanna sighed. Something told her she was making a mistake, but Peter did seem contrite, and she couldn't help how she felt about him.

"All right," she said, her expression softening. All of a sudden, being back in school again didn't seem half bad. It was hard to believe things had ever looked as bleak as they had that morning.

Obviously Peter *did* care about her. She must have been out of her mind to misjudge him so completely!

"You know, you really seem to be getting a feel for the stuff we've been reading," Elizabeth told Johanna, sitting back with an appreciative smile as she looked up from the essay Johanna had given her to read. The two girls were working after school together in the student lounge on Monday afternoon. "I think Mr. Collins is going to be impressed with this. It's clear that you understand the story, and your writing is much better, too—much clearer and more succinct."

Johanna gave Elizabeth a smile of gratitude. "I really want to pull it off this time," she said. "I'm so sick of feeling like the dummy. I want to be able to prove once and for all that I can make the grade—that I'm not slow." She shook her head. "I can't tell you how hard it was growing up in a musical family, Liz. No matter what I did, I just didn't measure up. In fact, even if I were able somehow to graduate with honors, I don't think my dad would really be proud of me. I still wouldn't have what it takes where it counts—in music."

"I'm sure your father doesn't feel that way!" Elizabeth cried. She couldn't imagine anything worse than feeling as if you had failed your parents. Surely Johanna was exaggerating her father's feelings. Elizabeth guessed the girl's strong feelings of inadequacy led her to perceive the situation the way she did.

But Johanna was adamant. "No one in my family has ever cared about anything but music." Her eyes filled briefly with tears. "My mother did, but now that she's gone, all my father and my sister talk about is music." She looked bitter. "And that definitely leaves me out in the cold."

Elizabeth felt a sudden wave of sympathy for Johanna. "What you're telling me just makes me admire your decision to come back to school all the more. What you've done takes real guts, Johanna."

Johanna sighed. "Well, maybe it did—at first." Her eyes shone. "Now I've got a goal. I want to prove to Peter that I can do well. I want to make him proud of me."

Elizabeth fiddled with the edge of her notebook. "So, did you end up going over to the DeHavens' yesterday when you left our house?" she asked, curious.

Johanna nodded. "He's *so* nice, Liz. He's just unbelievable to talk to. Whatever subject we end up on, it turns out he knows something about it. He's so interested in things, too. He subscribes to all these magazines, and he's always asking people questions, and you can just tell what a success he's going to be."

She looked wistful for a minute. "When I'm with Peter I get this feeling that I've never had before. I guess it's because he really feels like there's nothing in the world he can't do." She looked down at her hands, and when she looked up again, she had tears in her eyes. "Since my mom died, the world hasn't really seemed that way to me. It seems that one door after another has closed on me. Peter makes me feel kind of the way I used to when I was little—when I still believed everything was possible."

Not knowing what to say, Elizabeth patted Johanna's hand. Her heart went out to the girl, who struck her as unusually sensitive. She just hoped Peter was worthy of Johanna's feelings because Elizabeth couldn't stand the thought of her getting hurt.

Elizabeth had kept her promise to Johanna. She hadn't told anyone that Johanna was dating Peter—not Enid, not even Jeffrey. Only Jessica, and Jessica had sworn on her honor not to tell a soul. And Elizabeth trusted Jessica, but she didn't trust Peter DeHaven. She didn't think he was actually a bad guy, but she *did* think he was self-absorbed. And she had an uneasy feeling that Johanna might be investing her heart unwisely.

"Hi!" Johanna called as she let herself into the Porters' house. "Am I too late to help with dinner?"

70

"You can set the table," Julie called from the kitchen. "I made beef stroganoff, Dad's favorite," she added as Johanna entered the kitchen.

Johanna struck her forehead with her hand. "I completely forgot. Dad's coming back from San Francisco tonight!"

"I thought you might have forgotten," Julie said, stirring the beef stroganoff. "I was afraid you'd be late. He should be home any minute."

Johanna hurried to the adjoining dining room. She went over to a cabinet and took out their best tablecloth. "I'm really sorry. I was working with Elizabeth Wakefield. She was looking over an essay I wrote for Mr. Collins."

"You really seem to be working hard," Julie observed, standing in the doorway. "How is it coming? Do you feel like it's getting easier?"

"It is," Johanna said. "Actually, things are going pretty well." She smiled. "And it's fun to be back at school. Are you going to the dance this Friday?"

Julie looked surprised. "Yes, I'm going with John Pfeifer." John was the sports editor of *The Oracle*, and he and Julie had been friends for a while. They often went to school dances together. "Why?" she asked.

"Oh—I just wondered," Johanna smoothed the tablecloth over the table and took three plates out of the cupboard.

"Are *you* planning on going?" Julie asked.

Johanna shrugged. "I'm not sure. I'm kind of hoping Peter will ask me," she admitted.

71

"Peter!" Julie exclaimed. She looked upset. "Jo, I told you—he's going out with Amy. I know for a fact he asked her to the dance ages ago."

Johanna felt her face redden with anger. "How do you know?" she demanded. "You always act like you know everything! Hasn't it occurred to you that I have a better sense of what's going on between Peter and Amy than you do?"

"I'm only trying to keep you from getting hurt," Julie said, upset.

But Johanna was close to tears, and now that she had started, she couldn't stop herself. "You *always* do this!" she cried. "You always act like you're so darned superior, just because you get good grades and you're a musician. Well, I'm sick and tired of it! Just for once I want to have something of my own, something that you can't claim to be an expert about."

Julie was about to respond when the key turned in the front door. She headed toward the hallway, followed by Johanna. Dr. Porter hurried in, his violin case in one hand, a suitcase in the other. "Hey," he exclaimed, setting the cases down, "don't I get a welcome home hug from my two favorite daughters?"

"Dad!" Julie cried. She hurried forward and threw her arms around his neck.

But Johanna was too upset to control herself a moment longer. The sight of her father was all it took to reduce her to tears, and the next minute she was racing away, sobbing. She could

72

hear her father's distressed questions and Julie's soothing responses behind her, but she didn't bother to try to make out what they were saying. She fled to the safety of her room, where she could close the door and cry her heart out in privacy.

She had never felt so lonesome before, so completely misunderstood. The scene with Julie just reinforced her conviction that she mustn't give up on Peter.

She needed his affection terribly. And somehow she was going to win his love and respect.

Eight

"Cara, you look like you've lost your best friend,"
Lila Fowler commented, unwrapping her straw
and taking a sip of diet soda. Lila, Cara, and
Jessica were eating lunch together at one of the
tables on the sunny patio outside the school,
but Cara had barely said a word while Jessica
and Lila discussed at length what they were
going to wear to the dance on Friday night.
Jessica, as planned, was bringing Rob Atkins as
her date, and she was going to double with
Lila, who was also going with a guy from
Bridgewater.

"It's good advance planning," Lila had commented earlier. "After all, you know the Bridgewater Ball is coming up next month."

"What's the Bridgewater Ball?" Jessica had
asked, transfixed.

Lila gave her one of her scathing, don't-you-
know-anything-about-the-things-that-matter
looks. "It's *the* ball of the season. It's when

all the debutantes come out. You know what Bridgewater's like," she had added. "We're going to have to campaign to get invited." Bridgewater was a very exclusive suburb about twenty minutes away from Sweet Valley.

It struck Jessica now as a lucky coincidence that she had just happened to invite Rob to the Sweet Valley PTA dance. Perhaps he would know someone in Bridgewater who could get them tickets to the ball.

But Cara had shown absolutely no interest in the ball *or* the PTA dance. Not even Jessica's announcement that she had purchased the wonderful size-four dress from the mall seemed to cheer her.

"Hey, Cara, what's wrong with you?" Jessica asked her friend.

"Oh—I don't know," Cara muttered, pushing her tuna salad around on her plate with her fork. "I guess I'm just upset about Steve."

"Why?" Jessica asked innocently. "Is anything wrong?" She couldn't help feeling a tiny twinge of guilt, but she reminded herself that both Cara and Steven would thank her in the long run.

"I can't understand it. All of a sudden we seem to be having communication problems. We keep getting into these ridiculous fights. He's convinced I've been seeing other guys, which is crazy. I think *he's* the one who's been cheating, to tell you the truth. Anyway, last night I was so miserable I just didn't care anymore. I figured I'd just go ahead and invite him to the dance on Friday. And he got really angry! He started saying I should go with one of the guys I've been seeing!" Cara's dark eyes filled with tears. "I don't even know what he's talking about. What guys? You two know I haven't gone out with anybody but Steven!"

"Maybe," Jessica said judiciously, "that's part of the problem. Don't you think so, Lila?"

"It could be," Lila said vaguely, opening the latest issue of *Glamour* and thumbing through it.

"*I* think you ought to give Steve something real to worry about," Jessica advised. "Look, Ken Matthews doesn't have a date yet for the dance. Why don't you ask him to go with you? That'll teach Steve!"

Cara looked dubious. "But if he's already jealous," she began doubtfully, "won't it—"

"Trust me," Jessica insisted. By now she was certain Steven and Cara weren't right for each other. If their relationship had been solid she assured herself, her little machinations would never have worked.

"Well, I *do* want to go to the dance," Cara admitted. She looked across the patio to the table where Ken was sitting. Ken was a handsome, athletic blond. He was captain of the Sweet Valley High football team and a lot of fun. "I guess I might have kind of a good time with Ken," she murmured.

"Of course you will!" Jessica declared. "Now,

go over and ask him right now, before someone else nabs him or he asks someone."

She couldn't help feeling a sense of satisfaction as Cara got up obediently from the table and threaded her way around the tables toward Ken. Jessica knew her brother well enough to be almost certain that if Cara went to the dance with Ken, it would be the last straw.

It seemed appropriate to Jessica that she should be the one to break Steven and Cara up. After all, she had been the one who had tried to get them together in the first place. She had made a mistake, but now she was making up for it. They were lucky they had Jessica Wakefield to watch out for their welfare!

Johanna ate lunch quickly, then went to the library. She wanted to do some additional studying for her French class. She was intent on a series of French verb conjugations when the door to the library opened and Amy Sutton came in with several other cheerleaders—Robin Wilson, Jean West, Sandra Bacon, and Maria Santelli. They were all in uniform, as there was going to be a pep rally that afternoon before the soccer game. Amy, especially cute in her red-and-white uniform, just seemed so at home, as if she owned the school. She was the sort of girl Johanna had always feared and resented. Not that Amy was such a good student, but she always did well enough to get by. And she was so obviously in with the right crowd, so confident, so oblivious of people on the outside. Like Johanna.

"I just can't wait till Friday night," Amy declared in a normal voice, ignoring the library rules, which insisted people talk only in whispers. The librarian was away from her desk, though, and there was no stopping Amy. "I think the party I'm having is going to be fantastic. Robin, you're bringing George, right?"

George Warren and Robin had been dating for a while, and Robin nodded, putting her finger to her lips and pointing at Johanna to show she was trying to study.

Amy tossed her blond hair back imperiously. "I've invited *tons* of people," she said, even more loudly. Johanna felt as if Amy were staring straight at her. "*Everyone's* coming," she repeated.

"Come on, Amy, let's get the book you want and get out of here," Jean whispered.

Amy shot a reluctant look back at Johanna. "Oh, all right," she said. "I have to meet Peter anyway. He just goes *insane* if I'm late."

The group moved back into the bookshelves, and after a lot of whispering and giggling Amy apparently located the book she wanted, checked it out, and the four girls left Johanna to herself. It was no good, though. She couldn't concentrate on the verb conjugations. All she could think about was Amy's party on Friday night and the PTA dance. She imagined Amy and

Peter slow dancing together, and a lump formed in her throat. Finally she gathered her things together, jammed them into her backpack, and hurried out of the library. She just couldn't keep her mind on her homework when she was so distraught. Her French was just going to have to wait.

To her surprise, Amy and her friends were standing just outside the library, still talking animatedly. Peter had joined them and seemed to be listening to something Amy was telling him. He barely looked up as Johanna walked past. If he saw her, he didn't register it.

He acted as if he hadn't seen her, as if she didn't exist. *Because I don't exist for him,* Johanna thought numbly, her eyes filling with tears. *I was out of my mind to think it could possibly be different.*

Suddenly the walls seemed to be closing in around her, and once again a feeling of frustration and despair overcame her. In the old days, before she had left school and come back again, she would have skipped out when this happened. Gone for a walk, hopped on a bus, and gone downtown—anything to get out of the building. But Johanna refused to run away this time. She wasn't going to give them all the satisfaction of watching her fail.

Teeth clenched, she made her way down the hall to the student lounge and opened her French book again. She was going to make it this time. She had promised herself, and she was going to make it—however much it hurt.

*   *   *

"Johanna!" Peter called, hurrying across the parking lot to catch up with her. "I've been trying to find you all day," he added. "Where have you *been?*"

Johanna shrugged. "I've been around," she said coolly. "You've just been busy, Peter. Every time I see you, you're deep in conversation with Amy."

Peter jammed his hands in his pockets as he fell in step beside her. "We need to talk," he said, looking so earnest and sincere Johanna felt her anger beginning to dissipate. "Can I give you a ride home? Is that where you're going?"

Johanna nodded.

"Let me drive you," Peter begged her. "Come on, Johanna. I feel terrible about everything. Just give me a chance to explain."

"All right," Johanna murmured, slinging her backpack over her shoulder and following Peter across the lot to the spot where his car was parked. She wished she trusted him more than she did, but she couldn't help thinking that it figured he was offering her a ride *now*, while Amy was cheering at the football game. She got into the car.

As if he were reading her mind, Peter turned to her before putting his key in the ignition. "I don't blame you for wondering what's going on," he said quietly. "The truth is, Amy is much more involved in this whole thing between us than I realized. I'm really afraid of hurting her. The fact is, I promised to take her to the dance weeks and weeks ago, and help her out with the party she's giving beforehand. I guess I feel I should wait until after the dance to talk to her."

Johanna didn't say anything at first. "Well, I guess what you do with Amy is your business," she said. "It's just, well, after the other night . . ."

"I had a wonderful time, too," Peter said. "In fact, I can't remember the last time I had so much fun. You're really different, Johanna. You really *listen* to me."

Johanna fiddled awkwardly with the seat belt. She couldn't help wishing their conversations hadn't been so one-sided so far. It was true that she loved listening to Peter; she loved hearing about his plans, loved the enthusiasm he felt for everything. But she wished he were a little more sensitive to *her* feelings. Why didn't he ever ask her any questions about herself?

"I really care about you," he added gently, putting his hand over hers and squeezing it.

Suddenly Johanna's anger evaporated. This was Peter, after all. She had known him practically all her life. Why couldn't she let herself trust him, at least a little?

"I'm sorry," she mumbled. "It's just kind of hard for me, coming back to school and everything. Maybe I'm blowing things out of proportion."

Peter looked relieved. "Just as long as you don't hate me," he said, turning the key in the ignition. "Hey," he added suddenly, "why don't you come back over to my house, with me? We could just hang out for a while and talk."

Johanna thought of going back to her own house, which she knew would be empty. "OK," she said happily. She couldn't believe how much better she felt, knowing everything was all right between Peter and her again.

Ten minutes later he had parked the car in front of the DeHavens' pretty Spanish-style house, which was built around a central courtyard that Mrs. DeHaven had turned into an exotic garden. On Sunday, when she had visited Peter, they had spent most of the time outside. Johanna hadn't been in the house since she was little so Peter gave her a tour. Almost every room had something of Peter's in it—tennis trophies in the family room, photographs of him in the hallway, rows of special science books in the library. It was obvious how proud of him his parents were, and Johanna couldn't help feeling a little wistful as she looked around. She thought that if Peter came over to the Porters' house, nothing there would look as though it belonged to Johanna. It all looked like Julie and her father, and that made her feel sad.

But Peter soon cheered her up. He had so much energy, and he was so much fun. They spent hours going through old scrapbooks and photo albums, and soon Johanna felt as though she knew more about Peter's life than she had ever dreamed possible. Occasionally the nagging voice in her head reminded her that he still hadn't expressed much interest in *her* life. But Johanna had so little confidence she couldn't blame him. What had she really done that warranted much interest?

"Hey, is this the program you're writing for the science fair?" Johanna asked, coming across a notebook and a set of diskettes on the desk in the study while Peter was putting away the scrapbooks. She picked up a printout entitled "Sample Program: Practice Run" and scanned it with interest.

"Oh, yeah. You wouldn't be interested in that," Peter said.

Johanna gave him a quick glance. Actually, she had always loved computers. Before she worked at the Whistle Stop, she had worked for a couple of months in an office downtown, doing secretarial work. She had had full use of a personal computer, and when she wasn't word processing her boss's letters, she had fooled around with the computer and had actually written a few programs of her own. But she didn't tell Peter; she was sure he would think it was a joke.

The concept behind Peter's "psychologist" program looked fairly simple to her. The idea was that each question had to be answered with a "yes" or "no." Each positive response would require a set of additional questions on the same issue, whereas each negative response would elicit the next category of questions. Johanna had seen a documentary on a similar program recently and said as much to Peter, but he didn't seem to hear her. He was trying to line the photo albums up exactly as they had been, and he obviously wasn't listening.

Johanna sighed as she set the printout back down on the desk. Why would Peter care what *she* had to say about his computer program? After all, he had experts helping him, like his friend in Las Palmas. The last person he would listen to would be someone like her, so incompetent she could barely make it through the nonaccelerated courses at school!

Still, she felt hurt. She wished Peter would stop talking about himself long enough to listen to *her* for a minute, at least long enough to realize that even if she wasn't a superbrain, she had feelings, too.

"There!" Peter said, looking with satisfaction at the neatly rearranged albums. "How about if I drive you home now?" he added, turning to Johanna at last.

Johanna sighed. There didn't seem any point in being upset. Peter was Peter, and she was obviously being silly to expect an overachiever to care about anyone as ordinary as she was!

Nine

It was fourth period Wednesday morning, and Mr. Russo, the chemistry teacher, faced his class and frowned. Well known as the strictest and most demanding teacher in school, he was famous for his hard tests, and he was in the process of handing back an especially difficult one. "I want to say a few words about these tests before handing them back," he said, clearing his throat and running his hand through his hair. "I really am concerned about most of you. I haven't seen scores so low in years. My sense is that almost none of you really understands electromagnetic configurations—that is, no one but the one student who got an A on the test, who should count herself out of this. Johanna Porter, I think you deserve to be singled out." He gave her a smile. "In fact, your classmates may be a little irritated with you because you kept the curve high. You got ninety-two points out of one hundred. Congratulations."

Johanna felt her face burn. At first she couldn't believe her ears. She hadn't thought she had failed the exam, but she couldn't believe she'd gotten an A, either. As she stood up to take the exam from Mr. Russo, the whole class looked on with surprise and admiration. Johanna was embarrassed, but she also felt proud. For the first time in her life, she was being singled out because she had done so well, not because she'd failed. For the rest of the hour she felt a warm glow all over.

"Johanna," Mr. Russo said after the bell rang and everyone was gathering up books and papers and hurrying to the door, "can you stay after class for a minute? I'd like to talk to you."

Johanna felt shy as she approached his desk. "I can't believe this," she murmured, looking down at her exam with the big red A on it. "I've never gotten an A on anything before!"

Mr. Russo looked at her thoughtfully. "You know, I've been talking to Ms. Taylor, your math teacher. She says you're doing unusually well in algebra, and she thinks it's possible that if you took precalculus in summer school, you might be ready for the regular calculus course next year. Along the same lines, I think you have a real aptitude for science as well. I'm surprised it wasn't detected earlier. In any case, I don't see any reason why you couldn't, with a little extra work this summer, get yourself into advance placement physics next year. Who knows," he added, smiling kindly at her. "You might want to concentrate on math or science in college, and you'll find these courses a big help if you do."

Johanna's face lit up. "I really like math and science," she admitted. "I guess it's just that in my house, if you didn't know anything about music, it didn't count. No one in my family really cares that much about science," she admitted.

"Well, you know, pure math is much closer to music than most people realize," Mr. Russo told her. "Anyway, you and I should talk more about this. In the meantime, I think you should have access to the labs and the computer rooms during your study hall and after school. I want you to feel free to continue working at your own pace. You mustn't feel as if the rest of the class is holding you back."

Johanna thanked him. She could hardly believe what she had heard, and the more she mulled it over as she left the room, the more astonishing it seemed.

She felt almost triumphant. *Mom would've been so proud*, she thought. And for the first time since her mother's death, her memory didn't bring tears to Johanna's eyes. It almost felt good to remember her and to think how happy this would have made her.

Johanna Porter had finally done something right. She could hardly wait to find Peter to tell him what had happened!

*   *   *

"I'm really glad you and Rob can come to my party," Amy Sutton said to Jessica, running a comb through her blond hair and looking with satisfaction at her reflection. The girls had just finished an aerobic workout in gym class and were putting on their makeup in the locker room. Everyone else had gone, but Jessica and Amy were dawdling. "Do you think Cara and Steven will be able to make it?"

"Oh, Cara isn't going with Steve. She's going with Ken Matthews," Jessica said casually, outlining her eyes with blue pencil.

Amy looked surprised. "Why? Is something wrong? I thought Steve was around this whole week."

"Oh, he is. It's just they were really in a rut," Jessica remarked. "You know how it is. You start seeing someone, and then things get more and more obsessive, and sooner or later— well, the spark is gone."

"Who felt that way, Cara, or Steve?" Amy asked.

Jessica giggled. "To tell you the truth, neither of them. I have to admit, I kind of pulled a few strings, dropping a little hint here, another little hint there."

Amy's blue eyes widened. "You mean you deliberately tried to split them up?" she asked in astonishment.

Jessica shrugged. "I was the one who got them together in the first place," she reminded Amy. "I couldn't split them up if their relationship was very stable, could I? Anyway, you can never tell while you're right in the middle of something that things have gotten stale. That's what friends are for," she added complacently.

Amy looked horrified. She and Jessica had been good friends ever since the Suttons moved back to Sweet Valley, but Amy hadn't seen many of Jessica's schemes in action. Clearly this one wasn't to her liking. "It's one thing getting two people together. But deliberately breaking Steve and Cara up, just because *you* think they're 'stale' . . ."

Jessica didn't like the reproachful look Amy was giving her. Come to think of it, she didn't like Amy's attitude at all. "I wouldn't concern myself about it," she said lightly, dropping her eye pencil into her quilted makeup bag. She couldn't resist taking a little jab, so as she walked away she added, "Besides, I'd think you have your own share of problems, with Peter running around behind your back like he's been doing lately." There was a stricken expression on Amy's face. Peter was her first steady boyfriend at Sweet Valley High, and she was incredibly jealous of other girls. Jessica knew she shouldn't say anything more; Elizabeth had made her swear not to tell a soul that Peter and Johanna had been seeing each other. But she had to get even with Amy for criticizing her plan to break up Steven and Cara.

"What do you mean? Who's Peter seeing?" Amy asked, spinning around to face Jessica.

"Johanna Porter," Jessica said flatly. "It's all over the whole school, Amy. I can't believe you haven't heard by now."

Amy turned white. "I'm going to kill him," she seethed, grabbing her bag and racing out of the locker room.

Jessica sighed. Just one more reason to stay out of a relationship, she thought sorrowfully. Look at all the trouble it seemed to cause!

Catching up to Peter in the cafeteria and pulling him aside to an isolated corner, Amy said furiously, "Peter DeHaven, I want to know exactly what's going on between you and Johanna."

Peter stared at her. "Nothing," he said, obviously taken aback.

"Don't try to deny it. I happen to have heard from a *very reliable* source that you two have been seeing each other behind my back." Amy shuddered. "How could you? Couldn't you at least do a little better than Johanna Porter? The girl can barely spell her own name!"

Peter paled, but didn't defend Johanna. "Who told you they saw us together?" he asked, stalling for time.

"That doesn't matter," Amy snapped, crossing her arms and glaring at him. "I want to know why you're cheating on me, Peter."

By now Peter had partly regained his composure. "Amy, for heaven's sake," he said. "Keep your voice down," he added, looking nervously around them. "I haven't been *seeing* Johanna," he added. "Not in the way you think, anyway.

She and I are old friends. Naturally when she came back to school I made an effort to help her out. I mean, the girl needs help! I was trying to give her a hand with her chemistry, that's all. Don't make such a big deal out of it, Amy."

Amy looked uncertain. "You're sure that's all it was? You were just helping her out?"

Peter pressed his advantage. "Come on," he said. "You really think I'd be interested in Johanna Porter?"

That seemed to impress Amy. She thought it all over for a minute and decided Jessica must have exaggerated things. Who knew what Jessica was up to? Maybe she wanted to break Amy and Peter up now that she was through with Steven and Cara. "OK," Amy said. The next minute her temper flared again. "But I'm warning you, Peter. If I so much as see you talking to that girl, we're through! You understand?"

Peter sighed heavily. He understood Amy's meaning, all right. What he didn't understand was why he didn't just tell her to get lost. He hardly even enjoyed Amy's company. Sure, she had a lot of status around school. She was friends with all the right people, she was a cheerleader, she was really pretty. But their relationship seemed shallow to him. Amy wasn't a real friend. They barely even knew each other!

And Johanna. His heart ached when he thought about Johanna. She was so vulnerable, so *real*. Something was really there when he talked to her. He knew if he gave himself half a chance, he could come to care about her.

But he hadn't given himself a chance. Worse, he hadn't given *her* a chance. He talked nonstop about himself when they were together, feeling the whole time that all he really wanted was to cut all the nonsense, take her in his arms, and drop his defenses. He did want to know about Johanna's feelings. He wanted to ask her how she had managed to pull herself together after her mother's death, how she'd found the courage to come back to school.

But he couldn't do it. He just couldn't, and he didn't know why. He knew Johanna was just about the best thing that had ever happened to him, and he was throwing away the chance to be with her for Amy Sutton, whom he barely liked.

Peter made an excuse to leave Amy and hurried down the main corridor to Johanna's locker. He took out a sheet of loose-leaf paper, scribbled the following note, folded it up, and pushed it through a slit:

Dear Johanna:
Amy has found out about us somehow. I don't know what to do, but I'm afraid it's going to be impossible for us to see each other again. I'm sorry. Peter.

Johanna read the note twice, her expression incredulous. How in the world had Amy found out? The only people who knew she had been seeing Peter were Julie and Elizabeth Wakefield. And there was no way Julie would have said anything. Not in a million years. They were sisters, and Julie wouldn't hurt her—not in *that* way—for the world.

That left Elizabeth. But Elizabeth couldn't have done that to her!

Johanna's fingers trembled as she folded the note and dropped it into her backpack. All of a sudden her victory in chemistry seemed meaningless. Peter was what mattered, and clearly she had failed there, as she always failed.

Her eyes were so blurry with tears she barely noticed at first when she bumped into Elizabeth in front of the drinking fountain.

"Hi, Johanna! I heard you did really well on your chemistry test—" Elizabeth began.

Johanna cut her off, tears spilling over. "Don't be such a phony," she said angrily. "I know you told Amy about Peter and me, Liz. There's no point denying it."

Elizabeth was astonished. "What?" she cried. "Johanna, what on earth are you talking about? I would never do a thing like that!"

"Well, I don't see how else she could've found out," Johanna said, wiping the tears from her eyes. "Anyway, it's all over now. I'm giving up," she added, her eyes flashing. "I don't belong here, chemistry or no chemistry. I just end up messing up everything I do."

"Johanna, where are you going? Elizabeth

gasped, hurrying after her as she stormed down the hall.

"I'm leaving," Johanna said, her mouth set in a hard line.

"Leaving for *where*?" Elizabeth demanded.

Johanna turned to face her, and Elizabeth couldn't believe how cold and hard her eyes looked. "Who knows?" she said. "Maybe the Whistle Stop, or maybe someplace else. Anywhere but here!" With that, she hurried down the hallway, opened the main door, and disappeared.

"Jessica Wakefield," Elizabeth panted, hurrying across the parking lot to catch up with her twin.

Jessica was just opening the door of the Fiat. Her blue-green eyes were all innocence as she turned toward Elizabeth. "What is it?" she asked, unperturbed. "I'm kind of in a hurry, Liz, so if—"

"Forget your hurry," Elizabeth said angrily, her eyes flashing. "I have a question for you, and I want a straight answer. Somehow Amy Sutton found out about Johanna and Peter, and I want to know *how*."

Jessica thought fast. "I don't know what you're talking about," she said, stalling for time. An expression of feigned anguish crossed her pretty face. "Liz, I certainly hope you're not trying to imply that *I* had anything to do with it!" she cried.

Glaring, Elizabeth folded her arms. "Then how did Amy just happen to figure it out? Jessica, only two people knew what was going on, and since I know *I* didn't say anything—"

Jessica could see she was losing the battle. "OK, OK," she muttered. "I admit it, Liz. I *did* say something. But give me a break before you jump down my throat!" she added hurriedly, putting her hand up when she saw the furious expression on her sister's face. "I couldn't help it, Liz. Honestly! Amy practically forced me to tell her. In fact, she *did* force me."

"How could she force you to tell her if she didn't know a thing about it?" Elizabeth asked, incensed.

Jessica looked hurt. "You don't have one teeny little bit of faith in me, Liz. How would you like it if I treated you the way you're treating me now? Can't you at least give me the benefit of the doubt long enough to hear my side?"

"Go on," Elizabeth said. "And this had better be good."

Jessica took a deep breath. "It was for Amy's own good," she said rapidly. "Honestly, Liz, you would have done the exact same thing I did if you'd been in my shoes. Just listening to that girl going on and on about Peter was enough to break my heart! I really felt I owed it to her, as her *friend*, to clue her in before she made too big a fool of herself."

"Didn't you think you owed it to *me* to keep the secret I trusted you with?" Elizabeth demanded.

Jessica blinked. "Of course I did," she said. "Liz, don't be mad at me! I can't stand it when you look at me that way! You're right," she added, backing down when she realized there was nothing left to do but to apologize. "Say you forgive me, Liz, and I promise I'll do anything you ask. I'll do the dishes every single night next week. I'll let you have the car anytime you want forever and ever. I'll—"

"Stop," Elizabeth groaned, putting her hands over her ears. She hated herself for relenting, but somehow, no matter how determined she was to stay angry with her twin, she always ended up backing down. "You've really got me in a bind," she muttered unhappily. "I don't think Johanna is ever going to speak to me again."

Jessica was as contrite as Elizabeth had seen her in ages. "Let me make it up to you," she begged. "Ask me for a favor. Ask me to do anything, and I promise I'll do it!"

Elizabeth sighed. "The only thing I want right now is for Johanna to find some way to work out her conflict and stay in school," she said sadly. "I guess it isn't your fault everything's such a mess, though I do wish you hadn't gone back on your word."

"I'm sure everything will work out in the end," Jessica said cheerfully. "Come on, Liz. Brighten up! We've got the dance to look forward to Friday, and Amy's party beforehand."

"Yeah," Elizabeth said dully. "I guess we do."

She didn't see how she was going to be able to enjoy herself, knowing Johanna would be sitting home alone. But there didn't seem to be anything she could do, except hope against hope that Johanna would be tough enough to make it at school without Peter DeHaven's support.

Ten

Amy's predance party was in full swing by seven o'clock on Friday evening. The Suttons had gone out, and the living room was filled with snacks and cold drinks—everything to get the evening off to a great start. But Elizabeth got the distinct impression that no one was having that good a time. The atmosphere was strained, no doubt because Amy herself seemed to be in a rotten mood. She looked pretty as ever in a peach-colored jumpsuit, but her expression was sour, and she wasn't making her guests feel at ease.

"Count up the number of people here who seem to be mad at each other," Elizabeth murmured to Jeffrey.

Jeffrey's green eyes twinkled. "OK," he said, scanning the room. "Well, I think we have to start with your brother and Cara," he said judiciously. "Who's that girl Steven's with?"

"Oh, that's Eve Young," Elizabeth said, frowning. "She's a friend from college. Personally, I think he's come tonight on purpose just to keep an eye on Cara. Look at the way he keeps staring at her and Ken."

"So who's your candidate for most mad at each other?" Jeffrey asked teasingly, putting his arm around her and pulling her close to him. "Not you and me, I hope."

Elizabeth giggled. "Not unless you did something rotten that I don't know about," she assured him. "Well, I guess next in line might be Amy and Peter. They look like they're about to kill each other."

"Amy looks like she's about to kill *everyone*," Jeffrey agreed. "You think she and Peter are having a fight?"

Elizabeth shrugged. "Who knows? She and Jessica don't seem to be on friendly terms, either," she added suddenly, watching her sister walk past Amy as though she didn't see her. Elizabeth couldn't help giggling again. "Boy, this dance tonight looks like it's going to be loads of fun!"

Jeffrey's face suddenly turned serious. "I feel so bad about Johanna Porter," he said with a sigh, watching Julie come in with John Pfeifer. "From what you told me, she really needed a lot of support from people like Peter. And support is the last thing she got!"

"I wish she were going to be here tonight," Elizabeth agreed. "I can't believe she really intends to drop out again, just when she was doing so much better."

Looks like ambush coming our way," Jeffrey said. Sure enough, Jessica was hurrying toward them, a tall blond boy right behind her, who, Elizabeth guessed, must be Rob Atkins from Bridgewater.

Jeffrey was right. Any further talk about Johanna was going to have to wait until they were somewhere more private.

"I absolutely love this sort of thing," Lila Fowler declared, opening a makeup kit the size of a handbag and ruffling through it. Lila, Cara, and Jessica were in the girls' bathroom off the main corridor closest to the gym, where the PTA dance was being held. "It's so—you know, *primitive*. Nothing like dancing right where we had gym class this morning to make you feel really romantic."

"Don't be sarcastic," Jessica admonished her. "I think they've done a great job. The gym looks wonderful. The PTA had festooned the walls with posters and streamers. The Droids, Sweet Valley High's own rock band, had set their instruments up on a platform at one end of the gym and were playing to the cheers and excited cries of their classmates. The lights were dimmed, and a magical feeling was in the air. Jessica didn't care if the dance wasn't in some exotic ballroom; she loved dancing, and Rob was turning out to be a lot of fun.

"Just wait till the Bridgewater Ball," Lila crooned. She finally found her compact.

"What about you, Cara? Are you having fun with Ken?" Jessica asked.

Cara, who was dressed in a pair of tight black jeans and a sparkly T-shirt, seemed to be ready to cry. "Who *is* that gorgeous girl with Steve?" she asked gloomily. "And does she *have* to drape herself all over him all the time?"

"You're not supposed to be watching Steve. You're supposed to be having fun on your own with Ken," Jessica said, fluffing up her hair and admiring her leather miniskirt and skimpy white top in the mirror. "Come on, you two. Let's go back out. I want to hear The Droids' new song."

"How can I possibly have a good time with Ken when Steven's dancing every single dance with that—that—"

"Eve," Jessica filled in for her, as they entered the gym. "Hey," she added in a low tone, "look at what Susan Stewart's got on. That girl must spend even more on her clothes than you do, Lila."

Susan Stewart, a pretty redhead in the junior class, was well known for her expensive clothes and hobbies. Lila, Cara, and Jessica didn't know her very well. She spent a lot of her time with the crowd in Bridgewater, though her boyfriend, whom she was with that night, was Gordon Stoddard from Sweet Valley High.

Lila sniffed. "Well, who knows where she gets the money?" she said in her snootiest voice.

Jessica suppressed a giggle. The Fowlers hadn't been wealthy until Lila's father struck gold in the computer industry, but Lila managed to act as though they'd been millionaires for generations. It was true, however, that a mystery shrouded Susan Stewart. No one knew her real identity. She lived in Sweet Valley with a wonderful, loving woman named Helen Reister, who had brought her up since she was a baby. But Helen wasn't Susan's real mother. All anyone knew was that Susan's *real* mother, whoever and wherever she was, was fabulously wealthy and sent big checks to Helen to provide her daughter with everything she wanted.

Inside the gym, The Droids started to play a slow song. Cara searched the dimly lit gym for Steven. Their gazes locked, and she felt her face redden.

"Hey, Cara, do you want to dance?" Ken asked, coming over to join her.

Cara continued to watch Steven. "No. No thanks, Ken. Not just now," she said apologetically.

Ken followed her gaze. "Look," he said, "why don't you go over and ask him to dance with you? You're not going to feel better until you two clear the air."

Cara took a deep breath. "Maybe I should," she said softly. "You're sure you wouldn't mind?"

"Who me?" Ken said and laughed. "No, you go ahead, Cara."

Summoning up all her courage, Cara crossed the dance floor until she was standing in front of Steven and his date. "Steven, I—uh, I was wondering if you'd—if you want to dance," she blurted out.

Steven looked solemnly at her. It was hard to tell what he was thinking, but the next minute he turned to Eve. "Would you mind?" he asked her.

Eve, who was a good friend and knew all about Cara, smiled. "Go right ahead," she said warmly.

The minute Steven took Cara in his arms she knew it was all going to be all right again. "God, I've missed you," she murmured.

"Me, too," Steven said huskily. "When I saw you come in here with Ken—"

"What about you?" Cara cried. "Who *is* that girl?"

Steven chuckled. "Just a friend," he said softly, resting his chin on the top of her head. "Cara, I never wanted to go out with anyone but you, and I never did. *You're* the one who suddenly had all these guys after you—and were responding, too—at least according to Jessica."

"Jessica!" Cara exclaimed, her eyes widening. She pulled back from Steven to stare at him. "Was Jessica the one who told you I wanted to go out with other guys?"

"Yes, I guess so," Steven said slowly, an expression of understanding crossing his face.

"Uh-oh," he said. "I have a terrible feeling we've been duped."

"We've been Jessica-d," Cara said. "Steven, when I get my hands on that girl . . ."

"So you never wanted to go out with other guys at all?" Steven asked.

Cara shook her head. "Just you," she assured him. "And you didn't feel like all the spark was going out of our relationship?"

Steven groaned, pulling her close to him again. "That girl has gone too far this time," he muttered.

Because for now all that mattered was that they were back in each other's arms. It had all been a misunderstanding, and not even Jessica Wakefield had been able to do any real damage to their relationship. As Cara said later, after they had explained everything to Eve and Ken and managed to salvage what they could of the evening, to have a Jessica-proof romance was something to be proud of!

Cara could tell Steven was angry at Jessica, and she was upset, too. How could her best friend do something like this? There was only one way to find out.

"Uh-oh," Jessica said, setting down her soda. She was standing next to Lila at the bar when she saw Steven and Cara, hand in hand, coming toward her. Neither was smiling.

"Time for me to get lost," Lila said cheerfully. She walked off and left Jessica alone.

"Jessica, we want an explanation," Cara began.

"More than an explanation—we want revenge!" Steven growled.

Jessica gulped, thinking fast. "I was only testing you two," she improvised. "I figured if you *really* loved each other, you'd never fall for any of that stuff I said."

"You're going to have to do better than that," Steven said.

But Cara looked thoughtful. "She's right, Steve. *We're* really the ones at fault. We should have trusted each other."

Steven's eyes softened. "Maybe you're right," he said huskily, slipping his arm around her.

Jessica breathed a sigh of relief. Fortunately they were so pleased to be back together again that neither wanted to stay angry at her for long. She was off the hook—at least for now!

Elizabeth and Jeffrey were sitting with Elizabeth's best friend Enid Rollins and Scott Long, her date, at one of the big round tables set up in the corner of the gym, enjoying themselves immensely as they watched their friends on the dance floor. They had been dancing almost all night and were glad for a brief respite. Most of the other tables were full, and Elizabeth knew they couldn't count on being alone much longer. Other couples were gradually dropping out to sit on the sidelines and watch. But Elizabeth couldn't help being disappointed when Amy Sutton headed their way with Peter DeHaven and a crowd of Amy's friends behind her. "Looks like we're about to lose our peace and quiet," Elizabeth murmured to her friends.

"Mind if we join you?" Amy asked, putting her purse down next to Elizabeth and sitting down before she could answer. "Boy, I'm really exhausted," she added, fanning herself with her hand. "Did you see us out there?"

"No, I didn't," Elizabeth said, giving Jeffrey a wink. Just what they needed when they were tired, she thought—Amy Sutton! She couldn't believe she had ever had a real friendship with this girl. Amy had turned into such a vain, silly creature!

"Well, I think tonight was a lot of fun," Amy continued. "Don't you guys think so?" she asked, turning to Enid and Scott.

Enid nodded. "Your party was wonderful," she said with effort. There was no love lost between Enid and Amy, and Elizabeth suppressed a smile at the flat sound of Enid's voice.

Peter was looking hard at Elizabeth. "Hi, Liz," he said at last. "I haven't seen you in a while."

"No, I guess not," Elizabeth murmured.

"Liz, haven't you been helping Johanna Porter with her English?" Lila Fowler asked. "I hear she's been doing really well. Someone in her chemistry class said that Mr. Russo gave her the only A on the test they just took."

Elizabeth looked quickly at Peter to see what kind of reaction he would have to this information, but his expression remained blank.

"Yes, she *is* doing well," Elizabeth said quietly, letting it drop at that.

But Amy apparently couldn't stand hearing Johanna being complimented. "You mean Johanna actually got an *A* on a chemistry test? She must've cheated," she said coldly.

Elizabeth felt her face burn with anger. She watched Peter again to see his reaction, and she thought she saw him flinch, but he remained silent.

"Amy, that's a terrible thing to say," Elizabeth said flatly. "Unless you have some reason to suspect Johanna of being dishonest, you really shouldn't make remarks like that."

Amy didn't respond, but from the speed with which she changed the topic of conversation, Elizabeth assumed she had made her point. She could tell Peter was upset, but not until they were all getting up from the table did she get an opportunity to talk to him alone.

"I can't believe you could just sit there and listen to her say things like that about Johanna," Elizabeth said angrily to him. Amy had wandered off to the ladies' room, Lila and her date were getting their coats, and Jeffrey was talking to Aaron Dallas about their soccer game.

Peter flushed. "I—I couldn't help it. I just didn't know what to say."

Elizabeth was angry now. "Don't you realize how much Johanna looks up to you? She's desperate for encouragement. Here she is, practically killing herself to do well. She comes back

107

to school and risks total humiliation—and people like Amy make sure she feels rotten, instead of proud of herself. And people like you. . . ." Elizabeth dropped the rest of the sentence, afraid she was going too far.

Peter turned pale. "I know what you're saying," he whispered. "I've really let her down, haven't I?"

"I just don't understand you," Elizabeth said, her aquamarine eyes narrowing. "If you care for Johanna, why treat her the way you have been? And if you don't, what's the point in leading her on?"

Peter stared at her, a helpless expression in his eyes. But Elizabeth was too angry to carry on the discussion. "Just remember," she said in a low voice. "Johanna has been a good friend to you. I hope you can say you've been a good friend to her." With that she turned away, leaving Peter alone to brood about the events of the evening.

Eleven

Johanna turned over the page of the history book she was supposed to be studying for the quiz Mr. Fellows was giving that afternoon. Her heart wasn't in it, though. It had taken an incredible effort to come to school that morning. Mondays were always hard, but that morning. . . . She just couldn't really see the point in working hard, in studying, in trying to get through. What difference would it make in the end? At least at the restaurant she had friends, people she could joke around with, people who liked her and accepted her for what she was. School seemed terrifyingly cold and lonely.

She knew there was no point in thinking about Peter anymore. She hadn't heard from him all weekend, not since he'd left the note in her locker. She knew he had taken Amy to the dance, but in her heart she had been hoping he'd call her on Saturday and tell her it was all a mistake—that he still wanted to see her.

There was no point in fooling herself any longer. Julie had been right. Peter had never cared about her at all, and the sooner she admitted that to herself, the better.

The door to the lounge opened, and Johanna's stomach flipped over when she saw it was him. It was so hard, having to be at school, where she ran into him all the time! If only he'd just disappear. Every time she saw him she felt as if her heart were breaking.

"Oh, hi," Peter said, coming over to her. He looked slightly embarrassed, but as always he was very much in control of the situation. "Did you get my note?" he asked after an uneasy pause.

Johanna nodded. She didn't see what she could say about it, so she didn't say anything.

Peter cleared his throat. "I—uh, I'm sorry about everything. It's all such a mess," he added, giving her his most charming, genuine smile.

Johanna stiffened. "It's OK," she said, shrugging and turning back to her book.

Peter sat down across from her, watching as she flipped to the correct page. "We can still be friends," he said after a long silence.

Johanna looked up briefly from her book. "Yes," she said quietly. "We can still be friends, Peter." She couldn't help thinking that he didn't seem like a friend to her, not the way he'd been acting since she came back to school.

But Peter seemed vastly relieved, as if a weight had been dropped from his shoulders. "Well," he said cheerfully, getting up again and pacing around the room with his hands in his pockets. "You know, I've run into a glitch in the program I'm writing. I'm really not sure what I'm going to do. I've got the first two parts down OK, but the third part—it's on love and intimacy—just doesn't seem to be working."

Johanna suppressed a smile. *That figures*, she thought. *Typical Peter DeHaven. Everything is wonderful until you get to the love and intimacy part.* But she kept her face straight as she listened to a lengthy description of the problem. Apparently the "psychologist" was supposed to ask a series of increasingly complicated questions about the "patient's" ability to love, to form relationships, to trust and depend on others. The problem arose at the beginning of the question set. Peter wanted the program to ask if the "patient" were seeing anyone special. If the patient said "yes," one set of questions should follow automatically. But in this instance, if the patient said "no," some of the same questions still needed to come into play. It was getting very complicated. For one thing, he wanted the program to be able to ask if the "patient" had been seeing someone recently, or wanted to but just couldn't meet the right person.

"You know," Johanna said, getting interested despite herself, "I saw something like this on *NOVA* once. They had a diagram they had drawn up that looked a little bit like a tree. Each question paired off into two possible answers, and each answer paired off again, and again. Maybe you could try using a tree diagram to help you plot the program from the beginning."

Peter laughed. "That sounds a little simple, Johanna. This is for the science fair, remember?"

Johanna felt the color drain from her face. She turned back to her history book, speechless.

She couldn't believe Peter could be so rude. Just because he was so much smarter than she was and knew so much more about science, what made him think he could be so dismissive when she had been genuinely trying to help?

She didn't look up again from her history book. As far as Johanna was concerned, Peter could take his giant-size ego and his botched-up computer program and just disappear forever. She knew one thing: She never wanted to see him again. And she wasn't one bit sorry when he left the lounge, closing the door firmly behind him.

Johanna didn't know how it had happened, but apparently the rumor that she and Peter had been sneaking around behind Amy Sutton's back was all over school. Julie had warned her that people were talking about it at the dance. Apparently a number of people had overheard her accusing Peter of going out with Johanna. This was just the sort of information that spread like wildfire, and Johanna was aware all day that people were giving her strange, knowing little looks. At lunchtime a sophomore named Alicia Benson stopped her in line to ask how everything was going. "At least now that *Peter's* tutoring you, you should be all right," she added slyly. Johanna's face had turned bright red.

But the worst moment of all came during gym class. Johanna was late, because she had been in the office, filling out yet another set of forms. Starting school again seemed to be a bureaucratic headache on top of everything else. By the time Johanna got to the locker room, it was deserted—or so she thought. Everyone else was already in the pool. Johanna hurried over to her locker, opened it hastily, and began searching for her swimsuit. Only then did she realize that two girls were talking on the other side of the lockers. They obviously hadn't heard Johanna come in and had no idea they were being overheard. It took a second, but Johanna was able to place the voices. They were Lisa Howard and Yvonne White.

"I really can't believe it," Lisa said. "What on earth would Peter see in Johanna?" Granted, she's pretty. But she probably can't understand a word he says!"

Johanna froze, holding her swimsuit in her hand. She didn't know what to do. Her intuition told her to make a loud noise, do *something* to keep them from going on. But she didn't seem capable of moving so much as a muscle.

"I know what you're saying," Yvonne agreed.

"Believe me, I wouldn't have thought it was possible either. But Amy told Lila and Caroline the whole terrible story. Apparently she was so mad she said she almost *killed* him. I mean, it's bad enough having your boyfriend cheat on you. But Johanna Porter—"

"I know!" Lisa exclaimed. There was a sound of rattling, as if she were fitting her padlock on her locker door. "That's the ridiculous part of it. You'd think Peter would've tried to find someone a little closer to his own speed!"

"He sure couldn't have found anyone dimmer if he tried," Yvonne added.

Johanna felt as if she couldn't breathe. It was like having the wind knocked out of her. *Don't let them see me,* she prayed. *Don't let them walk over this way. I'll die if they know I heard them.*

To her immense relief, the girls strolled out through the showers to the swimming pool, leaving Johanna alone. She could hear their voices growing fainter and fainter, but—thank heavens—she could no longer distinguish the words.

Johanna sank down on a bench, her swimsuit dangling from her hand. She couldn't remember ever having felt this terrible before. Did she really appear to be so stupid to people? Why? Was it just because she'd dropped out? Because her grades had been bad?

Gradually, the terrible shock and hurt she felt began to be replaced by anger. Yvonne and Lisa had no right to talk about her that way.

OK, so she might not have had the greatest grades in the past. That had all changed. Johanna knew she could make it if she wanted to. Wasn't that all she had come back to school to prove?

But the fact that she could make it didn't change the way she felt at Sweet Valley High. It didn't make her any less of an outsider.

They weren't going to accept her no matter what she did, however many exams she managed to do well on. Peter hadn't accepted her, had he? He hadn't even taken her seriously enough to ask her anything about herself. All she had been to him was a good audience.

Well, she was through. Once and for all, through. They could forget all their stupid reentrance forms down in the office, because she had made up her mind: She was going to leave, and she wasn't coming back.

She knew she could walk right back into her job at the restaurant, and that was exactly what she intended to do. At least there no one would talk about her meanly. They actually looked up to her there. They were real friends.

Tears blinding her eyes, Johanna slammed her locker shut with trembling fingers. The next minute she was racing out of the locker room and down the hall, toward the main door—and freedom.

Twelve

Elizabeth couldn't believe her ears. "You mean she's gone? She really left?" she asked, dumbstruck.

Peter nodded. "I just bumped into Julie, and she told me she ran into Johanna this afternoon. She said she wasn't going to her next class, that she was going home. Julie said she was really upset. Julie couldn't get the whole story out of her, but apparently—he fidgeted—she overheard something in the locker room this afternoon that upset her. Some girls were talking about what had happened between us, and I guess they said some terrible things about Johanna."

Elizabeth's aquamarine eyes flashed. "They're not the first ones," she muttered. "God, when I think about what that poor girl has been through, I want to—" She abruptly stopped, then faced Peter. The two were out on the patio outside the cafeteria, and no one was within earshot.

"Did you say anything to upset Johanna today? Did you see her at all?"

Peter's brow wrinkled unhappily. "Yeah, I saw her in the lounge. She was working on some history, I think." He was quiet for a minute. "We didn't really say very much to each other. I mean, I talked for a few minutes about the computer program I've been working on, but that was it. She didn't say anything about herself."

"Did you give her a chance?" Elizabeth asked.

Peter dropped his eyes. "I guess not," he admitted.

"I don't understand you," Elizabeth said simply. "That girl has been so nice to you, Peter. Why not give yourself a chance to get to know her?" She searched his face. "Or is it safer sticking with Amy, whom you know you'll never really care about?"

She knew she had struck home, because Peter winced and looked away. "Look," he said at last, "I'm sorry Johanna's left school. But I really don't see what I can do about it."

"Sure, why should you worry?" Elizabeth said sarcastically. "You're all set! You've got your whole life mapped out—MIT, scholarships, science prizes. Why should it bother *you* that Johanna Porter's not going to finish high school because you, and people like you, never gave her the support she needed? Why involve yourself in someone else's problems when your own—" She stopped, trying to control her temper, then resumed, "When your own are so much *simpler*."

Peter stared at her. "What—what do you think she's going to do?" he managed at last.

Elizabeth shook her head. "She mentioned something last week about going back to waitressing at the Whistle Stop. That was the last thing she told me."

"Maybe I can call her up or something, let her know how bad I feel," he suggested lamely.

Elizabeth was so angry and upset she didn't think she could stand to talk to Peter for another minute. "Maybe," she said flatly. "Peter, I've got to go now. Do whatever you think is best."

With that she turned on her heel, leaving him staring blankly after her.

Peter hadn't taken the car to school that day, and his talk with Elizabeth had made him miss the bus. As he walked home he kept going over the conversation he'd had with Johanna that morning. He hadn't admitted it to Elizabeth, but he knew he'd been insensitive—for the hundreth time. He didn't know what it was about Johanna that made him act that way. All his life Peter had been socially graceful. He always knew just what to say, what to do to make people feel good. It was easy for him to make friends, and he knew people admired him and enjoyed spending time with him.

But he had never had a girlfriend before. Amy Sutton was the closest he'd come to having a steady girl, and he had to admit Elizabeth was right on that score: Amy wasn't an emotional risk. He knew she would never come to mean very much to him.

Johanna was different. He had never thought about her as anything but a close friend until she came back to school. She had grown so beautiful since he had last seen her. And it wasn't just that he was attracted to her, either. She had obviously grown up a lot since her mother's death. She had always been a warm, caring, friendly girl, but in the old days she didn't have much of an attention span. She got bored easily and couldn't commit herself to anything long enough to do well.

Peter could tell Johanna had changed, and the truth was that he felt threatened by her maturity. He knew how much she cared for him, and he was afraid that if he let himself, he would really fall for her. Fall in a way that he just wasn't ready for.

So he had backed off. He'd hung on to Amy, making sure she stayed between them. He had ignored every opportunity to get to know Johanna better and instead had filled up every minute of their time by talking about himself.

Peter felt deeply ashamed of himself. He knew he had treated her terribly. More important, she was in trouble now, and she had no one to turn to.

He felt he had to do something, but he didn't know what.

He was in his room, staring at the monitor of his computer and trying over and over again to work past the glitch in the program he was writing. He thought back to the suggestion Johanna had made that morning, and on a whim, he took out a pad of paper and drew a "tree" of questions and answers. Actually, the method turned out to be very useful. By charting the questions and answers so succinctly, he found the place where he had made the error.

Peter was overjoyed. It worked. It actually worked! His first feeling was one of triumph and relief. Now that the program was completed, he could write it up and send it in to the contest. He felt like celebrating—like going out to dinner or something. Excited, he hurried over to the phone to call Johanna. She was exactly the person he wanted to see. She would understand how wonderful it was that he had finally solved the problem!

Then he remembered, and his heart fell. They weren't even supposed to be speaking to each other, at least not according to that horrible note he'd left in her locker. He would call her and apologize.

The phone was answered by Johanna's father. "Johanna's not here," he said. "She's working at the Whistle Stop."

Dejectedly, Peter thanked Mr. Porter and hung up.

Suddenly he had an idea. *I'll just go over to the restaurant and apologize. That's all there is to it! I'll make her change her mind. She'll come back to school, and it'll be different between us. I'll make her believe that.*

He was convinced that if he put his mind to it he could make everything all right again. After all, Peter DeHaven had never failed at anything he really tried for.

And he wasn't going to fail this time, either.

"You can't be serious," Peter said. He was sitting in a booth in the Whistle Stop facing Johanna, who looked—even in the plain white uniform she was wearing—incredibly pretty.

Johanna's green eyes were steady on his. "I *am* serious," she assured him. "There's no way I'm coming back, Peter. I just couldn't stand it back in school."

"But you were doing so well! You never told me about Mr. Russo's test," he added, reaching across the booth to cover her hand with his.

Johanna pulled her hand back as if his touch burned her. "What was the point in telling you? You never listened to anything I said, anyway." Her voice cut him to the quick. It wasn't harsh or reproachful—it was matter-of-fact. She was stating the obvious, and that was what hurt the most.

"Look," Peter said, glancing around him with a desperate look on his face, "you don't belong here! You've got your whole life in front of you, Johanna. You're incredibly bright. You can do anything you set your mind to do. Why throw it all away?"

Johanna listened but didn't answer. Sensing he at least had her attention now, Peter pressed on. "Maybe I was a jerk," he added. "I never encouraged you. I never listened. Is that any reason to screw up *your* life? I don't see how that's going to punish *me*."

Johanna's eyes narrowed. "If you think I'm staying away from school because of you, you're wrong," she said rapidly. "You made it perfectly clear almost from the start that I shouldn't do things for you or because of you. Don't worry. You don't have to feel guilty about my decision, if that's why you're here."

Peter swallowed hard. He wanted to tell her he was there because he cared about her, because he thought he was falling in love with her. But the words seemed to stick in his throat. All he could do was look hopelessly at her, thinking how beautiful she looked—and how proud. What a jerk he'd been, he chastised himself. Johanna was undoubtedly the best thing that had ever happened to him, and he had ruined things between them. It seemed impossible to start from scratch.

"Well, whatever brought you out here, it isn't going to work. I'm happy here," Johanna said. "Nothing you say or do is going to change my mind, Peter." She looked up as her boss made a gesture toward a table in the corner. "Anyway, I've got to get back to work," she told him, rising from the booth.

As Peter watched her walk away, he felt a sinking sensation in his stomach. Much more was at stake here than his romance with Johanna. Her whole future was in the balance. But it was obvious there was nothing he could do. He was too late, and nothing he could say to her now could possibly make a difference.

Johanna came back from her shift absolutely exhausted that night. Julie had already gone to bed, and Dr. Porter was sitting alone in the living room, a book lying open on the couch beside him. He had his glasses off, and he was rubbing his eyes when Johanna came in.

"Hi, Dad," she said, dropping down into the leather armchair with a sigh. "I guess Julie told you that I bombed out again and that I went back to work at the Whistle Stop."

Dr. Porter put his glasses back on and paused a minute before answering. "She told me how unhappy you've been," he said gently. "Johanna, I wish you could have let me know. I wish"—he sighed—"I didn't feel like we've all become such strangers since your mother died."

Johanna felt a lump forming in her throat. "Mama wanted me to go back and finish," she whispered. "I found her journal in the attic, and I read it. I probably shouldn't have, but I did. She wanted me to go back."

Dr. Porter leaned forward, his chin in his hands. "Is that why you did it? For your mother?" he asked gravely.

Johanna nodded, tears coursing down her cheeks. "I didn't want to let her down. And now I have," she said brokenly.

Dr. Porter crossed the room and knelt to fold Johanna in his arms. "Listen, honey," he said, stroking her hair. "I don't blame you for feeling the way you did when you read that journal. But that doesn't change the fact that you've got to start doing things for *yourself*. That's what your mother always wanted for you. She knew Julie had her music, and what she hoped was that you would find something of your own to work for."

Johanna lifted her face, which was streaked with tears.

"I always felt that if it wasn't music, you didn't think it counted," she said sorrowfully.

"Oh, honey," Dr. Porter said, "nothing in the world could be further from the truth! You know," he added, taking a handkerchief out of his pocket and passing it to her, "I got a letter today from Mr. Russo, your chemistry teacher. He told me about the mark you got on your test, and he said he thinks you have an unusual aptitude for science. He'd like to see you enrolled in some special courses this summer to enrich the regular program. He thinks you're something special, Johanna."

Johanna dried her eyes with a tissue. "I guess I went back with the wrong motivation," she whispered. "It was wrong to try for someone else. First I wanted to do it to prove I could, for Mama's sake. And then there was Peter DeHaven. I thought if I could show him I was bright, he'd fall in love with me. And I found out"—she shivered—"I guess I found out he can't really love anyone. Not now, anyway."

Dr. Porter put his arm around Johanna. "Your mother always used to say you had a gift for people, Jo. She used to say Julie had music, and you had love. And she used to say she thought you were the lucky one."

Johanna's eyes filled with tears again. "I miss her," she said, fighting to keep the tears back.

But she needn't have tried. "So do I," her father said slowly. And the next minute they were crying in each other's arms.

Thirteen

Johanna waited until the following morning to tell her father and Julie her decision. Both her father and her sister were up early, as always, enjoying some peace and quiet before the day's routines got under way. Johanna had woken early as well. In fact she barely had slept. All night long she kept turning things over and over in her mind, going back over the events of the past month, trying desperately to understand what path she should take now.

It seemed to Johanna that her fundamental mistake had been believing, as her father put it, that she could—and should—do things for other people, and not for herself. Going back to school had to be an entirely self-motivated act. Her error had been to look for praise and support from others. Her mother wasn't there anymore, and even if Johanna knew in her heart that what she was doing would have pleased her, that was no reason to carry on—not unless she really wanted it herself.

And then there was Peter. Johanna was angry with herself for allowing herself to be so vulnerable to him, but she saw now that what she had done was to look to him for reassurance of her success. Peter hadn't been very supportive. That much was true. She believed he had treated both her and Amy unfairly, but she had been wrong to expect as much from him as she had in the first place.

No, she saw now that what she needed was to go back *on her own terms*, not for her mother, not for Peter, but for herself. The truth was that over the course of the past few weeks, Johanna had been truly excited about her math and science classes, especially science. And Mr. Russo believed in her. It wasn't music, but maybe that was even better. Science would be something all her own, and she knew she needed schooling—and lots of it—to forge ahead.

Johanna dressed with special care that day, her mind already racing ahead to each detail that might present itself back in school. She hadn't burned any bridges behind her yet. She would have to explain her absence for the past few days, but she knew her father would help her on that score. She would want to talk to Mr. Russo about the kind letter he'd sent. And—this pained her more than a little—she would have to find Elizabeth Wakefield and apologize.

She was sure now that Elizabeth wouldn't have told anyone about Peter and her. And Elizabeth had been a big help to her. She deserved thanks, not censure.

But first she had to announce her decision to her father and sister. "Good morning," she said, coming into the breakfast room with a big smile on her face.

"Hey," Dr. Porter said, putting down his newspaper and taking off his glasses. "That doesn't look like the Whistle Stop uniform!"

Julie's face lit up. "Are you coming back to school?" she asked, jumping up to engulf her in a huge hug.

Johanna took a deep breath. "I am," she said. "And I want to thank you both for helping me so much while I thrashed around, trying to make the decision." Her green eyes twinkled. "Last night I couldn't sleep, so I came downstairs and fiddled around with Dad's computer for a while. I hope you don't mind, Dad," she added hastily, "but I made a kind of present for you two, and I want to show it to you."

"Mind? You're the scientist in the family." Dr. Porter laughed. He and Julie got up from the table, followed Johanna into the study, and watched with interest while she turned the computer on.

"I've written a computer program for you," Johanna told them with a smile. "It's fairly simple, but hopefully it'll be the first of many." She paused, and then began to touch letters on the keyboard in a certain order. Each key had been programmed to correspond to a musical note, and Dr. Porter and Julie listened with astonishment as Johanna "played" the first six bars of Beethoven's Fifth Symphony on the keyboard.

"See, I just wanted to show you that the music is still there, even if it looks like it's a world away," Johanna said softly. The next minute the three of them were hugging each other, laughing and crying at the same time. They were crying because that symphony had been Mrs. Porter's favorite piece of music, and for the first time the three of them were mourning her death together.

But at the same time they were all looking forward to the future together. They felt like a family again—a real family!

"Do you realize," Julie said, shifting her books from one arm to the other, "how long it's been since you and I walked to school together?"

"Remember when you started first grade? Mama made me walk with you, and I was embarrassed." Johanna smiled sadly. "I was a big cool second grader, and I didn't want to be seen dragging you with me."

Julie reddened slightly. "I guess we've taken turns being proud and ashamed of each other, sometimes with reason, sometimes not. Johanna, I never told you how proud I was of you when you decided to come back to school."

Johanna sighed. "There was so much you and I never said to each other, Julie. It seems to me that after Mama died, our whole house just kind of fell apart. We all turned into strangers."

"Still," Julie objected, "it was wrong of me not to encourage you more than I did. Maybe" —she looked uncomfortable—"I was a little nervous about having you come back. In any case, I feel I owe you an apology."

Johanna smiled, tucking her arm through Julie's. "I'll accept the apology," she said lightly, "only if you promise to help me with my history and English for the next few weeks. Something tells me I'm going to need a patient tutor. Elizabeth Wakefield has been wonderful, but I don't want to wear her out."

Julie giggled. "I promise to help—on one condition," she said. "You have to help me with chemistry and math. Do you know Mr. Harrison gave me a C minus on my last quiz?"

Both girls were giggling as they approached the entrance to Sweet Valley High. Johanna felt an incredible wave of relief as they climbed up the front steps together. For the first time she felt as if she and Julie were equals—just two sisters who had different interests, different strengths and weaknesses.

She felt closer to her sister than she had in years. The truth was, she felt proud of her— and proud of herself as well. It was a new sensation, and one that Johanna intended to savor!

"Johanna," Peter said, hurrying to catch up with her in the hallway. "I've been trying to find you all morning. I don't suppose you'll have lunch with me, will you?"

Johanna looked seriously at him for a minute, then smiled. "Sure, Peter," she said, "but it has to be quick. I promised Mr. Russo I'd meet him in the chem lab at twelve-thirty." She couldn't help thinking that a few weeks ago she would have jumped at the chance to have lunch with Peter. But everything had changed now. She couldn't believe she'd been back at school for only a month. She had apologized to Elizabeth, who had generously forgiven her. Now the two were beginning to be real friends, and through Elizabeth, Johanna had met some really nice girls. She wasn't lonesome anymore. Besides, she had tons of work to catch up on—so much that she didn't even have time to think about Peter anymore. At least not very much. She had heard through the grapevine that he had broken up with Amy, who still gave Johanna dirty looks every time they passed in the hallway. But Johanna hadn't really spoken to Peter since that afternoon in the Whistle Stop. He had made several attempts to talk, but each time she had made some excuse.

Once they had gotten through the cafeteria line and were actually sitting down together at one of the small tables on the patio, Johanna realized—with immense relief—that everything was going to be OK. It didn't hurt to see him again at all. And when he asked her how she was, she could say, quite truthfully, that things were going extremely well. She had taken some diagnostic tests in math and science, and as Mr. Russo had suspected, she tested out unusually high in both areas. Now he was helping her locate summer-school programs in precalculus and physics, and Johanna was even beginning to look into computer programming courses in California colleges. The future looked bright.

Peter listened to everything she said with obvious interest. "You know," he said at last, "I never thanked you properly for the advice you gave me on the program I entered in the science fair. You were right. The 'tree' method of mapping was exactly what I needed to do. In fact, I found out yesterday that I won! Only *we* won, really," he added. "I couldn't have gotten through it without your help."

Johanna was pleased for him, and told him so. "Maybe next year *I'll* try entering," she said, taking a bite of salad.

Peter looked at her admiringly. "You're really something, Johanna. I just want to tell you how proud I am of everything you've done this past month."

Johanna turned serious. "That's nice of you to say, Peter. I'm glad we're still friends."

Peter reddened slightly. "I was wondering. . . ." He fiddled with his fork. "Do you have plans for Friday night? I was hoping you'd let me take you out to celebrate the science fair victory."

Johanna was quiet for a moment. She couldn't help thinking that whatever Peter said, the science fair was *his* victory, not hers. She liked him, but she could see now that he was too wrapped up in his own achievements to be able to give of himself, at least for now. "I'm sorry," she said gently, "but I'm going to a concert with my sister." She grinned. "My dad is playing in Sweet Valley this weekend, and since he's my favorite violinist, I thought I'd make it my business to be there."

Peter was obviously disappointed. "What about Saturday?" he pressed her.

Johanna shook her head again. "I don't think so, Peter. I just don't really think it would be a good idea." She looked away, summoning up her courage. "I've got a long haul ahead of me, and to tell you the truth, I just want to concentrate on getting my own life back together for now. I have a lot of lost time to catch up on with my dad and sister. And I'm starting to make some real friends, too. I guess that's about all I can take on right now. I don't think I'm ready to think about guys and dating."

Peter looked hurt. "I messed everything up, didn't I?" he muttered, looking away.

Johanna felt a pang as she saw the hurt expression in his eyes, but there was nothing more she could say.

She had learned the hard way that she couldn't force something that wasn't there. She had taken a long searching look at herself and sorted through her priorities, and she knew now what she wanted.

Eventually she would meet someone who was able to give as much to her as she could give back. But Peter wasn't that special guy. And for now, she had her work cut out for her. If she really was going to win the science fair next year—on her own—then it was time to get cracking!

Johanna knew she was going to do it. The best thing was, she was going to do it because she wanted to. And she knew she was going to make herself proud!

"Well," Jessica said gloomily, pushing her lunch tray away from her, "it looks like Steve and Cara are much more in love than ever. My little plan to come to their rescue sure backfired."

She and Lila were in the cafeteria, catching up on gossip before classes resumed. But Lila wasn't paying attention to Jessica. Her eyes were fastened on Susan Stewart, who had just walked past, arm in arm with Gordon. As usual, Susan was dressed beautifully in an expensive-looking, stylish olive-green dress. The color suited her red hair and brown eyes. She looked great.

"You know," Lila said, leaning forward and lowering her voice. "I couldn't help overhearing Susan talking to Regina Morrow today in the bathroom. You should have heard the way Susan was going on about Helen!"

"Who's Helen?" Jessica asked with a frown.

"The woman she lives with, the one who's raised her," Lila said impatiently. "Anyway, Susan was going on and on about how Helen won't tell her who her real parents are." Lila's eyes were getting bigger as she relayed the story. "Susan said she couldn't wait to find out who her real mother was." Lila raised her eyebrows. "Do you think her mother really *is* someone famous, like everyone says?"

Jessica shrugged. "I think she must be. You can tell things like this just by the way a girl looks and carries herself," she added knowingly. "Susan Stewart is obviously incredibly highborn. Just look at her posture! Look at the way she dresses! She's got *class* written all over her! Mmmm." Jessica watched Susan smile at Gordon as he pulled a chair out for her. "The whole thing sounds like Cinderella, doesn't it?"

Lila nodded. "It does. The only question is how much longer is Susan going to have to put up with living in the cinders over on Trowbridge Street!"

Jessica giggled. Only Lila would call the modest suburban street where Susan lived "the cinders." True it wasn't the nicest part of Sweet Valley. The street was quiet and clean, but it wasn't in a wealthy section of town.

The question was, who was Susan's real mother? And how much longer would it be before she identified herself and solved the mystery?

Find out the answers to these questions in Sweet Valley High #37, RUMORS

A Favorite Sweet Valley High™ Super Edition!
Share the Magic of France with Jessica and Elizabeth!
Take off for Spring Break!

Jessica and Elizabeth are nearly bursting with excitement and anticipation, and you will be too, when Spring Break comes around—and they're off to the glamorous South of France! It's the vacation of a lifetime and Elizabeth can't wait to practice her French while Jessica, of course, is dying to meet those romantic French boys!

The Riviera turns out to be even more beautiful and wondrous than the twins had imagined, with its beach clubs, magnificent mansions, and the glittering Mediterranean Sea. But while the Frenchwoman with whom the girls are staying is a warm and welcome hostess, her handsome son René is arrogant and rude! Can the twins figure out why René seems to despise them or will he spoil their dream vacation?

Bon Voyage!

☐ SPRING BREAK: SWEET VALLEY HIGH Spring Super Edition #1 25537-1 $2.95
☐ SPRING FEVER: SWEET VALLEY HIGH 2nd Spring Super Edition #2 26420-6 $2.95

Buy them at your bookseller or use this convenient coupon for ordering.

It's the New Hit Series from
Bantam Books that takes you behind
the scenes of a T.V. Soap Opera.

Share the highs and lows, the hits and flops, the glamour and
hard work, the glory and heartache of life on the
Soap Set with:

KATIE	SHANA	MITCH
NOLAN	BRADBURY	CALLAHAN

Each a star in their own right, each a seasoned professional
aiming for the top, each a teenager dealing with the ups and
downs, the crazy ins and outs of teenage life—all in the glaring
light of the camera's all-seeing eye!

ALL THAT GLITTERS
It's *Golden!*

☐ **MAGIC TIME: ALL THAT GLITTERS #1** (26342 • $2.50)
☐ **TAKE TWO: ALL THAT GLITTERS #2** (26417 • $2.50)
☐ **FLASHBACK: ALL THAT GLITTERS #3** (26479 • $2.50)
Price and availability subject to change without notice.